生活英語

chit-chat 聊不停，
聽力會話好流利

USER'S GUIDE 使用說明

開口說英語,從日常生活開始學習,
就能清楚聽懂問話,也能輕鬆回答!

1 反映日常實況,多種情境設定

每一句會話、互動對話、聊天內容,都是老外實際生活的演練;不論表達情緒或互動溝通,亦能有兩種以上情況舉例反應……英語理解更透澈,輕鬆聽得懂、開口說。

EX:It's your turn.
(輪到你了。)

○ **換你了,加油:**

A: It's your turn. Good luck.
　輪到你了,祝你好運。

B: Thanks.
　謝謝。

○ **下一個輪到誰呀:**

A: Whose turn is it?
　換誰了?

B: It's your turn.
　換你了。

○ **終於輪到我了:**

It's your turn. Please come to the *stage*.
換你了,請你上台來。

2 生活單字一起記,更有效率

每一會話皆以使用最頻繁、你較熟悉的字彙來編寫;同時將「關鍵單字」精選出來再次溫故知新,學習壓力能降到最低,無負擔並有效地擴充扎實的字彙庫。

* bear	[bɛr]	動	忍受
* grief	[grif]	名	悲傷、感傷

3 Chat 不斷流，溝通更生動

全文在每 8-10 句的實境常用語學習之後，將其串連成一聊天小品，讓你更理解溝通時正確的使用時機及語言精髓，達到實戰開口演練並能活用學習成果。

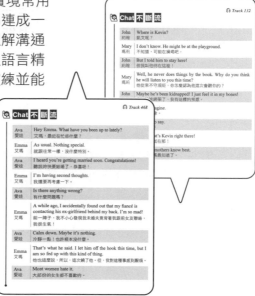

4 聽說能力，齊頭並進

全書常用語、會話對話、情境小品，皆附有專業外師語音檔，逐句錄音製成單一音軌，隨時想學哪一句、想聽哪一段，隨掃即聽超方便，時時都能浸淫在老外的生活氛圍裡。

PREFACE

現在的你,想學好英文的動機是什麼呢?除了學生因為考試,大部分的讀者都是在進入社會之後才感慨:「若是能夠有基本的英文溝通能力,一定能在工作上或生活裡更有幫助啊!」

能夠開口用英文溝通,是許多人希望能達成的目標!

沒錯,學英文,最重要的目的也就是為了要「能溝通」。我知道很多人都曾有想把英文學好的決心,但令人沮喪的是,明明在學校學了好多年的英文,但當真的要開口說英文或和老外溝通時,卻結結巴巴地擠不出完整的一句話……這一次,我們要給你絕不會放棄的信心!你的目的,就單純的只是「想要開口就能用英語表達」,那麼這一本《生活英語:chic-chat 聊不停,聽力會話好流利》,帶你用自學的方式,假以時日,一定能夠達成目標;重點是,特別精心設計以「生動活潑的情境編寫」方式,讓你覺得學習有趣,一定能「持之以恆」。

其實,想要開口說英文,真的一點都不難!像是我有一些外國朋友,也是在來到台灣之後才學中文的。他們也不是一開始就學ㄅㄆㄇㄈ,但仍能每天中文都說得更多一些、更進步一點,很快地就能開口用道地的中文跟我們溝通了。我覺得個中絕竅是:他們一點都不怕出糗或尷尬,現學現賣,不斷地從錯誤中學習、進步,才能讓自己的中文說得嚇嚇叫!學英文亦是同樣的道理,只要從現在開始行動,跟著這一本《生活英語:chic-chat 聊不停,聽力會話好流利》自學,每天學一點,再跟著音檔天天朗讀,相信很快地就真能用英文表達,自然地和老外閒聊、談天說地了。

相信自己一定做得到並立刻行動,就是邁向成功的一大步!加油~

CONTENTS

全書音檔雲端連結

因各家手機系統不同，若無法直接掃描，仍可以至以下電腦
雲端連結下載收聽。

（https://tinyurl.com/2m6wt637）

Chapter 1

- 日常點滴 -

Daily Life

Chapter 01 音檔雲端連結

因各家手機系統不同，若無法直接掃描，
仍可以至以下電腦雲端連結下載收聽。
(https://tinyurl.com/49jnatp3)

🐱 Chat 聊不停

01. **Have a nice day.**　祝你今天愉快。

💬 <u>一早心情愉快：</u>

A: Good morning.
早安！

B: Good morning. Have a nice day.
早安！祝你今天愉快！

💬 <u>祝福總使人好心情：</u>

A: Have a nice day!
祝你今天愉快！

B: Same to you.
你也是喔！

02. **Good afternoon.**　午安。

💬 <u>不要浪費美好的午後時光：</u>

A: Good afternoon, Joe. Where are you going?
喬伊，午安！你要去哪裡啊？

B: I am going to have tea with Peter.
我和彼特要去吃下午茶。

💬 <u>出來走走，吹吹風：</u>

A: Good afternoon.
午安。

B: Good afternoon. It's a beautiful afternoon.
午安。今天下午天氣真好。

Chapter **01** 日常點滴 *Daily Life*

03. The sun is scorching today.　今天太陽好大。

💬 **夏天總是豔陽高照：**

A: It's summer time!
現在夏天了。

B: Yes, the sun is scorching today.
對啊！今天太陽好大。

💬 **陽光太強，小心紫外線：**

A: The sun is scorching today.
今天太陽好大。

B: Then stay at home.
所以待在家吧！

04. How's the weather today?　今天天氣怎麼樣？

💬 **陽光普照的天氣：**

A: How's the weather today?
今天天氣怎麼樣？

B: It's sunny.
晴天。

💬 **熱得令人吃不消：**

A: How's the weather today?
今天天氣怎麼樣？

B: Very hot.
很熱。

05. I'll start as soon as possible.　我馬上開始。

💬 **到底什麼時候開始：**

A: When will you start singing?
你什麼時候開始唱歌？

B: I'll start as soon as possible.
我馬上開始。

💬 **肚子餓時總沒耐性：**

A: When will you start cooking?
　　你什麼時候開始做飯？

B: I'll start as soon as possible.
　　我馬上開始。

🎧 *Track 006*

06. Let's go shopping.　一起去逛街吧！

💬 **購物血拼最開心：**

A: There is a new shopping center down the street. Let's go shopping.
　　街上開了一家新的百貨公司，我們去逛街吧！

B: Oh, yeah!
　　耶！

💬 **有空嗎？一起出去逛逛吧：**

A: Let's go shopping!
　　一起去逛街吧！

B: Sorry, I can't. I still got a lot of work to do.
　　對不起，我不行。我還有很多事要做。

🎧 *Track 007*

07. Take it or leave it.　要就要，不要就拉倒。

💬 **不要再挑三撿四的了：**

A: Don't you have anything better than millk?
　　你沒有比牛奶更好的了嗎？

B: Milk is all I have. Take it or leave it.
　　我只有牛奶，要就要，不要就拉倒。

💬 **不能再便宜了：**

A: I'll buy it if you lower the price.
　　如果你降價的話，我就買。

B: No, take it or leave it.
　　不行，你要就要，不要就拉倒。

Chapter **01** 日常點滴 *Daily Life*

08. **After you.** 你先（請）。

💬 **禮讓是一種禮貌：**

A: Please come in.
請進。

B: After you.
你先請。

💭 **沒關係，讓你先：**

A: Let's go in there.
我們進去吧！

B: After you.
你先請。

09. **It's your turn.** 輪到你了。

💬 **換你了，加油：**

A: It's your turn. Good luck.
輪到你了，祝你好運。

B: Thanks.
謝謝。

💭 **下一個輪到誰呀：**

A: Whose turn is it?
換誰了？

B: It's your turn.
換你了。

💬 **終於輪到我了：**

It's your turn. Please come to the *stage*.
換你了，請你上台來。

* stage	[stedʒ]	名	舞臺、階段

10. **You've been there? 你去過？**

💬 **真的嗎：**

A: Disneyland is fun.
迪士尼樂園很好玩。

B: You've been there?
你去過？

💭 **你確定：**

A: Taiwan is fun.
台灣很好玩。

B: You've been there?
你去過？

🐾 Chat 不 斷 流

Sammy 珊米	Good afternoon. 午安。
Ben 班恩	Hey! How's the weather today? 嘿，今天天氣怎麼樣？
Sammy 珊米	The sun is scorching today. 今天太陽好大。
Ben 班恩	It's better to stay indoors on a day like this. 這樣的天氣，最好待在室內。
Sammy 珊米	Exactly. Let's go shopping! 沒錯，我們去逛街吧！
Ben 班恩	Sure. How about Taipei 101? 好，臺北 101 怎麼樣？
Sammy 珊米	You've been there? 你去過？

Chapter 01 日常點滴 Daily Life

Ben 班恩	Yeah. I've been there a few times. 是啊，我去過幾次。
Sammy 珊米	Let's go then. 我們走吧。
Ben 班恩	After you. 你先請。

🎧 *Track 012*

11. **Don't push me.**　別逼我；別推我。

💬 請小心一點，撞到我了：

A: Watch it! Don't push me.
注意！你別推我。

B: Sorry. 對不起。

💭 承受不了壓力：

A: Would you stop pushing me?
你可不可以不要逼我了。

B: Then give me back my money.
那你還錢來。

🎧 *Track 013*

12. **Now that's the way.**　這還差不多。

💬 乖乖順從：

A: OK. I'll go with you.
好，我跟你走。

B: Now that's the way.
這還差不多。

💭 知道分輕重：

A: I'll do my homework before I play.
我要先做功課再去玩。

B: Now that's the way.
這還差不多。

13. I have to *attend* a meeting later.　　等會我要開會。

💬 要開會了，走不開：

A: Want to go get a cup of coffee?
要不要去喝杯咖啡？

B: No, thanks. I have to *attend* a meeting later.
不，謝了，我等一下要去開會。

💭 分身乏術，能幫一個忙嗎：

A: Can you mail these letters for me? I have to *attend* a meeting later.
你可以幫我寄一下信嗎？我等一下要去開會。

B: Sure thing.
沒問題。

* at·tend	[əˋtɛnd]	動	出席

14. What are we going to do later?　　我們待會要幹嘛？

💬 太無聊了，找點樂子吧：

A: It's really boring just staying here. What are we going to do later?
待在這裡好無聊喔，我們等一下要幹嘛？

B: I don't know. Any ideas?
我不知道，你有什麼點子嗎？

💭 累到不想動了：

A: What are we going to do later?
我們等一下要幹嘛？

B: I don't know. I am all worn out.
我不知道，我好累。

15. May I have your name, please? 請問你叫什麼名字？

💬 詢問對方身份：

A: I have an *appointment* with Mr. Kin.
我和秦先生有約。

B: May I have your name, please?
請問你貴姓？

💬 有事先訂位：

A: I have reserved a table for two.
我訂了兩人的位子。

B: Yes. May I have your name, please?
是的，請問你的大名是？

* ap·point·ment	[əˋpɔɪntmənt]	名	預約

16. listen to... 聽……（的指示）

💬 鬧脾氣：

A: I won't listen to you anymore.
我不要再聽你的了。

B: Stop being a baby.
別再孩子氣了。

💬 做個聽話的孩子：

A: You should listen to your mother.
你應該聽媽媽的話。

B: OK.
好。

💬 請安靜，聽我說：

Can everyone just listen to me for a second?
大家可不可以先聽我一下？

17. As long as you're happy.　你開心就好！

💬 **要走的留不住：**

A: Will you let me go?
你會讓我走嗎？

B: As long as you're happy.
你開心就好！

💬 **你隨心所欲吧：**

A: Will you let me do that?
你會讓我做這件事嗎？

B: As long as you're happy.
你開心就好！

18. How long do you want us to wait for you?
你要我們等你多久啊？

💬 **動作可以快一點嗎？：**

A: I will be ready soon.
我馬上就好了。

B: How long do you want us to wait for you?
你要我們等你多久啊？

💬 **等太久了：**

A: How long do you want us to wait for you?
你要我們等你多久啊？

B: Five more minutes.
再五分鐘。

Chapter 01 日常點滴 *Daily Life*

19. *Lock* the door, please. 請把門鎖上。

💭 別忘了要關門：

A: I'm home. 我回來了。

B: *Lock* the door, please.
請把門鎖上。

💭 請對方順手關上門：

A: Can I come in?
我可以進來嗎？

B: Yes, but lock the door, please.
可以，但請把門鎖上。

* lock	[lɑk]	動	鎖上

20. It's really interesting. 太有趣了

💭 愉快的旅行：

A: How was your trip to New York?
你的紐約之行怎麼樣？

B: It was really interesting.
太有趣了。

💭 好書總是看不膩：

A: This book is really interesting. I have already read it twice.
這本書太有趣了，我已經看過兩遍了。

B: What is the title of the book?
書名是什麼？

💭 太好玩了！大推：

The game is really interesting.
這個遊戲真的很好玩。

🐾 Chat 不斷流

Bree 布麗	What are we going to do later? 我們待會要幹嘛？
Danny 丹尼	I have to attend a meeting later. 等會我要開會。
Bree 布麗	Really? On a Friday night? 真的？星期五晚上？
Danny 丹尼	Yeah. My boss wants me to talk to him about the upcoming project. 對，我老闆想跟我討論接下來的企劃案。
Bree 布麗	So tough! Why don't you quit? 太辛苦了，幹嘛不辭職？
Danny 丹尼	I love my job. 我很喜歡我的工作。
Bree 布麗	As long as you're happy. 你開心就好！
Danny 丹尼	Lock the door, please. 請把門鎖上。
Bree 布麗	Can we go out for a drink when you're done? 你結束後，我們能去喝一杯嗎？
Danny 丹尼	I don't know how late that's going to be. 不知道結束會不會很晚。
Bree 布麗	Listen to me, you really have to take a break once in a while. 聽我說，你偶爾必須休息。
Danny 丹尼	Don't push me anymore! 別再逼我了。

21. **It stinks.** 好臭！

💭 **習慣成自然：**

A: How can you eat your lunch here? It stinks!
你怎麼能在這裡吃你的午餐啊？這裡好臭喔！

B: I am used to it.
我習慣啦！

💬 **實在忍不住了：**

A: Who farted? It stinks.
誰放屁了！好臭喔！

B: Not me.
不是我。

💬 **臭得受不了啦：**

It stinks here. I want to leave.
這裡好臭，我想走了。

22. **I didn't** *notice*.　我沒注意。

💭 **心無旁鶩：**

A: Was that Tim who just passed us?
剛剛經過我們的是提姆嗎？

B: I didn't *notice*.
我沒注意。

💬 **看電影不要說話：**

A: Did you see the bad guy leave a note in Tom Hanks' pocket?
你有沒有看到那個壞人在湯姆漢克的口袋裡留了一張紙條？

B: I didn't *notice*. Please be quiet and let me watch the movie!
我沒注意！請你安靜讓我看電影。

* no·tice	[`notɪs]	動	注意

23. Are you wearing a new *outfit* today?
你今天穿新的衣服嗎？

💬 **感覺是第一次看見：**

A: Are you wearing a new *outfit* today?
你今天穿新的衣服嗎？

B: No, I bought it last year.
不是，我去年買的。

💬 **稱讚別人的新衣服真好看：**

A: Are you wearing a new *outfit* today? It looks really nice.
你今天穿新的衣服嗎？看起來很好看。

B: Thank you.
謝謝。

* out·fit	[ˋaʊtˏfɪt]	名	裝備、服裝

24. I lost my *wallet / purse*.　我的皮夾／錢包掉了。

💬 **咦！我的皮夾呢：**

A: Oh no! I lost my *wallet*.
糟了，我的皮夾丟掉了。

B: Don't worry. I will find your *wallet* for you.
別擔心，我會替你把皮夾找出來。

💬 **錢包掉了，沒有錢吃飯：**

A: I lost my *purse* and I don't have money to eat lunch.
我的錢包掉了，我沒錢吃午餐了。

B: Don't worry. I can pay for you.
別擔心，我可以幫你付錢。

💬 **錢包不見了，真倒霉：**

What a bad luck! I lost my *purse*.
運氣太差了吧，我弄丟了錢包。

Chapter 01 日常點滴 *Daily Life*

* purse	[pɜs]	名	錢包；女用手提包
* wal·let	[ˈwɑlɪt]	名	錢包；皮夾

🎧 *Track 027*

25. Could you give me a ride?　方便載我一程嗎？

💬 **就在附近，順路載我吧：**

A: Could you give me a ride? My house is only three blocks away.
方便載我一程嗎？我家只離這裡三條街區遠。

B: Sure. Why not?
當然，有什麼不可以。

💬 **能夠搭個便車嗎：**

A: I twisted my *ankle*. Could you give me a ride?
我的腳踝扭到了。你可不可以載我一程？

B: Where do you live?
你住哪裡？

* an·kle	[ˈæŋkl̩]	名	腳踝

🎧 *Track 028*

26. Your outfit is *dazzling*.　你的穿著好炫！

💬 **驚嘆他人的打扮：**

A: Wow! Your outfit is *dazzling*.
哇！你的穿著好炫喔！

B: Thank you.
謝謝你。

💬 **精心打扮，盛裝出席：**

A: Your outfit is *dazzling*.
你的穿著好炫喔！

B: It took me awhile to come up with what to wear to the party.
我想了好一陣子才知道要穿什麼來參加派對。

* daz·zle	[ˈdæzl̩]	動	眩目、眼花撩亂

🐾Chat 不 斷 流

Noel 尼爾	Hey, your outfit is dazzling. Are you wearing a new outfit today? 嘿，你的穿著好炫！你今天穿新衣服嗎？
Phoebe 菲比	Oh, yeah. I got them last week. 對啊，我上個禮拜買的。
Noel 尼爾	Awesome! 讚！
Phoebe 菲比	I think I am too fat. 我覺得我太胖了。
Noel 尼爾	I didn't notice that you've gained weight. 我沒注意到你變胖啊。
Phoebe 菲比	I am going on a diet. 我要開始節食。
Noel 尼爾	You don't even need to do that. 你不需要節食。
Phoebe 菲比	Thanks, but I am never happy with my body. 謝謝，但我從來都不滿意我的身材。

🎧 *Track 034*

31. I'm full / hungry. 我飽（餓）了。

💬 **再也吃不下了：**

A: Please eat more. 請再多吃一點。

B: I'm full already. 我已經飽了。

💬 **吃太少，很快就餓了：**

A: I'm hungry. 我餓了。

B: What did you eat for dinner? 你晚餐吃了什麼？

🎧

32. I'm so thirsty.　我好口渴。

💬 **想喝水：**

A: I'm so thirsty.
我好口渴。

B: So am I.
我也是。

💬 **吃不下，只想解渴：**

A: Want something to eat?
要吃什麼嗎？

B: No, I'm so thirsty.
不要，我口好渴。

💬 **誰有水嗎：**

I'm so thirsty now.
我現在口好渴。

33. I don't feel like eating.　我吃不下；我沒食慾。

💬 **一點都不想吃：**

A: Why didn't you eat dinner?
你為什麼不吃晚餐？

B: I don't feel like eating.
我沒有食慾？

💬 **別人關心你：**

A: What's the matter?
怎麼了？

B: I don't feel like eating.
我沒有食慾。

💬 **請求對方諒解可以這樣說：**

Please forgive me. I don't feel like eating.
請原諒我，我沒有食慾。

34. **I don't feel well.**　我不舒服。

💬 狀況看起來不大好：

A: You look *weak*.
你看起來很虛弱。

B: I don't feel well.
我不舒服。

💬 生病了：

A: What's the matter?
怎麼了？

B: I don't feel well.
我不舒服。

💬 撐不住了：

I don't feel well. I have to take a rest.
我不舒服，我必須要休息一下。

* weak	[wik]	形	無力的、虛弱的

35. **It never rains but it *pours*.**　禍不單行。

💬 壞事接二連三：

A: Yesterday I was hit by a car, and to make matters worse, I was robbed on my way to the hospital.
昨天我被車撞了。更糟的是，我在去醫院的途中被搶劫了。

B: It never rains but it *pours*.
真是禍不單行！

💬 真是太倒霉了：

A: I was late for school today. What's worse, I found that I lost my purse on my way to school.
我今天早上上學遲到。更糟的是，我發現我的錢包在上學的途中搞丟了。

B: It never rains but it *pours*.
真是禍不單行！

* pour	[por]	動	澆、倒

Chapter 01 日常點滴 *Daily Life*

36. could be worse　可能更糟

💬 不幸中的大幸：

A: I fell off the tree and *twisted* my ankle.
我從樹上摔下來，把我的腳踝扭到了。

B: You were considered lucky already. It could have been worse.
你已經算是很幸運了，情況有可能更慘。

💬 值得慶幸：

A: Ms. White gave us five reports to write.
懷特老師給了我們五個報告要寫。

B: You should be *grateful*. It could have been worse.
你應該覺得慶幸，有可能給的更多呢！

* twist	[twɪst]	動	扭曲
* grate·ful	[ˈgretfəl]	形	感激的、感謝的

37. Poor thing.　真可憐。

💬 表示同情：

A: She can't come here.
她不能來這裡。

B: Poor thing.
真可憐。

💬 哦，真令人擔心：

A: He is in hospital.
他在住院。

B: Poor thing.
真可憐。

38. What's the rush?　你趕著去哪裡？

💬 **急急忙忙地：**

A: Hey! What's the rush?
喂！你趕著去哪裡？

B: I left my books at home.
我把我的書放在家裡了。

💬 **快來不及啦：**

A: Larry, what is the rush?
賴瑞，你趕著去哪裡？

B: The train is going to leave in ten minutes.
火車再十分鐘就要開了。

39. Take it easy!　放輕鬆點！

💬 **緊張到手心冒汗：**

A: My palms are sweating.
我的手掌都流汗了。

B: Take it easy! You are going to be all right.
放輕鬆點，你沒問題的。

💬 **別擔心，一定能成功的：**

A: I don't know if I will be able to win the race.
我不知道我可不可以贏得比賽。

B: Take it easy! You can do it.
放輕鬆點，你可以的。

💬 **輕而易舉：**

Take it easy. It's not hard at all.
放輕鬆點，這一點也不難。

* palm	[pɑm]	名	手掌

Chapter 01 日常點滴 Daily Life

40. **Don't take things too hard.** 想開一點。

💬 **放輕鬆，沒那麼嚴重：**

A: Cheer up. Don't take things too hard.
  想開一點，別把事情看的那麼嚴重。

B: I know what to do.
  我知道該怎麼做。

💬 **沒什麼大不了的：**

A: I just can't take it anymore!
  我受不了了。

B: Hey! Relax! Don't take things too hard.
  放輕鬆！想開一點囉。

💬 **只是小事一件：**

Don't take things too hard. It's just an interview.
你該想開一點，這只是場面試罷了。

 Chat 不 斷 流

Tom 湯姆	Would you like something to eat? 你想吃什麼嗎？
Annie 安妮	No, thanks. I'm full. I don't feel like eating, but I'm thirsty. 不了，謝謝，我很飽，吃不下，但我很渴。
Tom 湯姆	I'll go get you some water. 我去拿點水給你。
Annie 安妮	Oh, I don't feel well. 我不舒服。
Tom 湯姆	Poor thing. Do you need to go to the doctors? 真可憐，你要去看醫生嗎？

Annie 安妮	No, it's fine. I'll just take some rest. 不用，沒關係，我休息一下就好。
Tom 湯姆	You must've been too stressed at work. Take it easy! 你一定是上班壓力太大了，放輕鬆點！
Annie 安妮	You're right. 你說的對。
Tom 湯姆	Yeah. Don't take things too hard! 是啊，想開一點！
Annie 安妮	Today is really not my day. 今天真不順。
Tom 湯姆	Come on, don't say that. It could be worse! At least you're not in the hospital. 別這麼說嘛，情況還可能更糟，至少你不用進醫院。

🎧 *Track 045*

41. Let's talk about it. 我們商量一下。

💬 **互相溝通決定方向：**

A: Where should we go on our first day?
我們第一天要去哪裡？

B: Let's talk about it first.
我們先商量一下

💬 **取得共識：**

A: What would we eat?
我們要吃什麼？

B: Let's talk about it first.
我們先商量一下。

💬 **計畫是要經過討論的：**

Let's talk about the plan for our summer vacation.
我們來商量一下暑假計畫。

42. **Let me think about it.** 讓我考慮一下。

💬 購物不能衝動：

A: Do you want to buy this?
你要買這個嗎？

B: Let me think about it.
讓我考慮一下。

💬 三思而後行：

A: Do you plan on going?
你有計畫要去嗎？

B: Let me think about it.
讓我考慮一下。

💬 遇難題要審慎思考：

Let me think about it. This question is not easy.
讓我考慮一下，這個問題不簡單。

43. **What then / How then / Where then?** 不然呢？

💬 覺得奇怪：

A: Why did you come here?
你為什麼要來這裡？

B: Where else then?
不然去哪裡呢？

💬 不是正常的狀況：

A: Are you out of your mind?
你瘋了嗎？

B: What then?
不然呢？

44. **It's disgusting!** 討厭死了；噁心！

💬 這部電影真令人反胃：

A: What do you think about the movie?
你覺得這部電影怎麼樣？

B: It's disgusting!
很噁心！

💬 可怕的讓人想吐：

A: Do you like snakes?
你喜歡蛇嗎？

B: It's disgusting!
噁心死了！

💬 啊～嚇死我了：

It's disgusting! There is a dead mouse.
噁心死了！有隻死老鼠。

45. **I feel like it.** 我高興（怎麼做就怎麼做）。

💬 任性妄為：

A: Why are you fooling around all day long?
為什麼你玩了一整天？

B: I feel like it.
我高興。

💬 不顧他人感受，任性妄為：

A: Why do you do that first?
為什麼你先做這件事？

B: I feel like it.
我高興。

Chapter 01 日常點滴 *Daily Life*

46. That's fine with me!　我沒意見。

💬 **怎麼樣都可以：**

A: What do you think of this?
你覺得這如何？

B: That's fine with me!
我沒意見。

💬 **你決定就好：**

A: I'll let him use your car when you're on vacation. Is that okay?
你去渡假時，我讓他用你的車，可以嗎？

B: That's fine with me!
我沒意見。

47. It depends.　看情形。

💬 **視情況需要而定：**

A: When will you wake up?
你什麼時候會起床？

B: It depends.
看情形。

💬 **不是想要就可以的：**

A: When will you buy a new car?
你什麼時候要買新車？

B: It depends on when I will have enough money.
這要看我什麼時候有足夠的錢。

48. supposed to　應該是

💬 理應在原來的地方呀：

A: Where are the books?
書在哪裡呀？

B: They are supposed to be on the shelf.
它們應該在書架上的。

💬 早該完成的事：

A: You were supposed to turn in the report yesterday.
你昨天就應該交報告了。

B: Oh, no!
糟了！

💬 很抱歉，沒有先告訴你：

I'm supposed to let you know first.
我應該先讓你知道。

49. by the way　順道一提

💬 隨口問：

A: By the way, where is the bathroom?
順道一提，廁所在哪裡？

B: Just around the corner.
就在轉角。

💬 只是順口提醒一下：

A: We are going to have a meeting this afternoon. By the way, are all the files ready?
我們今下午要開會，對了，資料都準備好了嗎？

B: Yes, they are all right here.
好了，它們都在這裡。

💬 附帶說明：

By the way, I'll call you back later.
順道一提，我等等會回電給你。

50. contact me　與我聯絡

💬 **對方不在，留下口訊：**

A: Ms. Lee is not here.
　　李小姐不在這裡。

B: Please tell her to contact me as soon as possible.
　　請她快點與我聯絡。

💬 **還沒有回應：**

A: Have you heard from Jet yet?
　　你有傑特的消息了沒？

B: He hasn't contacted me yet.
　　他還沒與我聯絡。

💬 **希望對方快點回應：**

Please contact me as soon as possible.
請盡快與我聯繫。

🐱 Chat 不 斷 流

Graham 葛拉漢	You were supposed to contact me last night. 你昨晚應該打給我的。
Nina 妮娜	I forgot. Sorry! 我忘了，抱歉！
Graham 葛拉漢	That's alright, but I need to talk to you about Amy. 沒關係，我想跟你談談艾咪。
Nina 妮娜	Can we talk about it now? 能現在說嗎？
Graham 葛拉漢	It depends. How much time do you have? 看情形，你有多少時間？
Nina 妮娜	I've got plenty of time. Let's talk about it. 我有很多時間，我們來討論一下吧。

Graham 葛拉漢	I really don't understand her. How can she be so vain? She is putting the whole company in jeopardy. 我真不懂她，她怎麼能這麼自大？她危害整間公司。
Nina 妮娜	I know. It's disgusting. 我懂，討厭死了。
Graham 葛拉漢	If the manager wants to fire her, I mean, that's fine with me. 如果經理想開除她，我沒意見。

🎧 *Track 056*

51. You decide.　你決定吧！

💬 沒意見：

A: What do you want to eat?
　　你想吃什麼？

B: You decide.
　　你決定吧！

💬 都可以，你喜歡就好：

A: Do you want the black tie or the red one?
　　你想要那條黑的還是紅的領帶？

B: You decide.
　　你決定吧！

Chapter **01** 日常點滴 *Daily Life*

52. **The most important thing is...** 最重要的是……

💬 三分天註定，七分靠打拼：

A: You are smart. But the most important thing is that you are *diligent*.
你很聰明，但是最重要的是你很用功。

B: Thank you.
謝謝你。

💬 全力以赴最重要：

A: You fail. But the most important thing is that you have done your best.
你失敗了，但是最重要的是你盡力了。

B: It's true.
沒錯。

💬 心腸好勝過長相美貌：

You are polilte. But the most important thing is that you are kind.
你很有禮貌，但是最重要的是你很善良。

* dil·i·gent	[ˈdɪlədʒənt]	形	勤勉的、勤奮的

53. **under normal *circumstances*** 在正常情況下

💬 稀鬆平常的結果：

A: Under normal *circumstances*, this will work.
在正常情況下，這個是會作用的。

B: Really?
真的？

💬 違反常理：

A: Under normal *circumstances*, he will listen to you.
在正常情況下，他會聽你的。

B: Maybe there is something wrong with him.
也許他發生了什麼事情。

💬 **如果沒有意外的話：**

Under normal *circumstances*, you can learn all these things in two months.
在正常情況下，你可以在兩個月之內學完所有的事情。

| * cir·cum·stance | [ˋsɝkəmˏstæns] | 名 | 情況 |

🎧 *Track 059*

---

54. You can say that again! / You said it!
你說得沒錯！／你說對了！

💬 **再同意不過了：**

A: That was the best concert I've seen.
那是我看過最好的演唱會！

B: You can say that again!
你說得沒錯！

💬 **事實確實如此：**

A: Your mom makes the best bread ever.
你媽媽做的麵包是最棒的。

B: You said it.
你說對了！

🎧 *Track 060*

---

55. Look who's talking!　看看你自己吧！

💬 **自己先照照鏡子：**

A: You should really go on a diet.
你真的應該要減肥囉。

B: Look who's talking! You have gained a few pounds yourself.
看看你自己吧！你也增加了幾磅啊。

💬 **龜笑鱉沒尾：**

A: Jimmy never finishes his food.
吉米每次東西都不吃完。

B: Look who's talking! You never finish your food, either.
你自己還不是一樣，你也不吃完你的東西啊。

56. **What would you like to eat?** 你要吃什麼？

💬 決定好了嗎：

A: What would you like to eat?
你要吃什麼？

B: I want some noodles.
我想要吃麵。

💬 也能這樣回答：

A: What would you like to eat?
你要吃什麼？

B: Hamburger, please.
漢堡，謝謝。

57. **It's better than nothing.** 有總比沒有好！

💬 將就一點吧：

A: I hate hot dogs.
我討厭熱狗。

B: It's better than nothing.
有總比沒有好！

💬 不要再挑剔了：

A: I hate this jacket.
我討厭這件夾克。

B: It's better than nothing.
有總比沒有好。

58. **Wait for me.** 等等我。

💬 慢一點：

A: You are going too fast. Wait for me.
你走太快了啦！等等我。

B: Then hurry up.
那麼你快一點啊。

不等你了哦：

A: We are going to leave now!
我們現在就要走了。

B: Hey! Wait for me!
喂！等等我啊。

再給我一點時間：

Wait for me please.
請等等我。

🎧 *Track 064*

59. The sky's the limit.　沒有限制。

預算無上限：

A: How much can we spend on books?
我們可以花多少錢買書？

B: The sky's the limit.
沒有限制。

勢在必得：

A: Are you sure you are going to pay any price for that house?
你確定你要為了那房子出任何的價錢？

B: Yup! The sky's the limit. I am determined to buy that house.
是的！毫無限制，我決心要買那棟房子。

🎧 *Track 065*

60. Why is there a traffic jam again?　怎麼又塞車了？

車禍影響交通：

A: Why is there a traffic jam again?
怎麼又塞車了？

B: There's a car accident.
那裡有車禍。

車流量太龐大：

A: Why is there a traffic jam again?
怎麼又塞車了？

B: There's too many cars on the road.
因為那裡有太多車在路上。

🧑Chat 不斷流

Quinn 昆恩	What would you like to eat? 你要吃什麼？
Rachel 瑞秋	I'd like a hotdog. 我想吃熱狗。
Quinn 昆恩	I don't think they've got hotdogs here. How about a burger? 這裡好像沒熱狗。漢堡如何？
Rachel 瑞秋	I don't like burgers. 我不喜歡漢堡。
Quinn 昆恩	You're so picky! 你真挑！
Rachel 瑞秋	Oh, look who's talking! 你有什麼資格説我！
Quinn 昆恩	You're so much pickier than I am. 你比我挑很多。
Rachel 瑞秋	Fine. You decide! 好啦，你決定吧！
Quinn 昆恩	Burger it is. It's better than nothing! 那就漢堡吧，有總比沒有好！
Rachel 瑞秋	Yeah. Get me one, please. 好吧，請買一個給我。
Quinn 昆恩	The most important thing is that we won't starve. 最重要的是我們不用餓肚子。

61. **My car broke down.**　我的車子拋錨了。

💬 不是故意的！事出有因：

A: Why are you so late?
你為什麼遲到那麼久？

B: My car broke down.
我的車子拋錨了。

💬 說明原委：

A: What happened?
怎麼了？

B: My car broke down.
我的車子拋錨了。

💬 始料未急的狀況：

It's annoying that my car broke down.
我的車子居然拋錨了，真是太煩了。

62. **My car has been towed.**　我的車子被拖吊了。

💬 車被拖了很無奈：

A: Where's your car?
你的車呢？

B: My car has been towed.
我的車子被拖吊了。

💬 只好搭公車了：

A: Why did you come by bus?
為什麼你搭公車來？

B: My car has been towed.
我的車子被拖吊了。

Chapter 01 日常點滴 *Daily Life*

63. I ran out of gas.　我的車子沒油了。

車子需要加油了：

A: Why are we at the gas station?
為什麼我們在加油站？

B: I ran out of gas.
我的車子沒油了。

車子沒油了，所以來晚了：

A: Why are you late?
你為什麼遲到？

B: I ran out of gas.
我的車子沒油了。

無預警的狀況：

I ran out of gas on the way.
我的車子在路上沒油了。

64. May I take you there?　我送你一程好嗎？

我載你去吧：

A: I want to go to school.
我要去學校。

B: May I take you there?
我送你一程好嗎？

要搭順風車嗎：

A: I want to go to the market.
我要去市場。

B: May I take you there?
我送你一程好嗎？

65. Be prepared.　準備好（要有心理準備）。

💬 **提前告知做好準備：**

Be prepared! She is a very strict teacher.
準備好喔！她是一個很嚴的老師。

💬 **理當如此的事：**

You should be prepared before you go to class.
你去上課之前應該要先準備好。

* strict	[strɪkt]	形	嚴格的

66. (It's) easier said than done.　說得比做得簡單。

💬 **用說的比較容易：**

A: To get good grades, all you have to do is study hard.
　　你只要用功讀書就可以得到好成績。

B: It is easier said than done.
　　說得比做得簡單。

💬 **知易行難：**

A: Relax! Don't be so nervous.
　　放輕鬆！別那麼緊張！

B: It is easier said than done.
　　說得比做得簡單。

Chapter 01 日常點滴 *Daily Life*

67. **That's easy for you to say.** 你說的倒容易。

💬 沒那麼簡單：

A: Remember to keep up your hard work.
記得保持你的努力喔！

B: That's easy for you to say.
你說的倒容易。

💬 不要只出一張嘴：

A: It's only a five-hour walk from here.
那離這裡只是五個小時的路程罷了。

B: That's easy for you to say. Then why don't you go?
你說的倒容易，那你為什麼不去？

💬 不然你來試試看：

That's easy for you to say. You should try once.
你說的倒容易，你應該自己試一次看看。

68. **Give me a break!** 饒了我吧！

💬 拜託，我也很忙的：

A: Can you help me with my homework?
你可不可以教我做功課？

B: Give me a break! I have a lot of work to do myself.
饒了我吧，我還有很多自己的事要做呢！

💬 撐不下去了：

A: It's only a twenty-minute walk.
那只是一段 20 分鐘的路程。

B: Give me a break! My legs are killing me.
饒了我吧！我的腿好痛。

💬 忍受不了了：

Give me a break! It's enough.
饒了我吧！真是夠了。

69. It's time to go. 該走了。

💬 **哇，擔誤太久了：**

A: Oh my God! I have lost *track* of the time. It's time to go.
天啊！我沒掌握好時間，我該走了。

B: OK. See you then.
好，再見囉。

💬 **時間到了：**

A: Hurry up! It's time to go.
快一點，該走了。

B: Just a minute.
再等一下。

💬 **快要來不及了：**

It's time to go, or we're going to be late.
該走了，不然我們要遲到了。

* track	[træk]	名	路線

70. We'll do as you say. 就照著你的意思做吧！

💬 **你決定：**

A: I want to go there.
我要去那裡。

B: We'll do as you say.
就照著你的意思做吧！

💬 **你說了算：**

A: I want this here.
我要放在這裡。

B: We'll do as you say.
就照著你的意思做吧！

💬 **你作主就好：**

It's your house. We'll do as you say.
這是你的房子，就照你的意思做吧！

🐾Chat 不 斷 流

Mandy 曼蒂	Oh no, I ran out of gas. I will be late for work! 噢不，我的車子沒油了。我上班會遲到！
Mitchell 米契爾	May I take you there? 我送你一程好嗎？
Mandy 曼蒂	That'd be great! 那就太好了！
Mitchell 米契爾	Alright. Hop in! It's time to go. 好，上車吧！該走了。
Mandy 曼蒂	Ew! There's a dead rat on my seat. 嗯！我的座位上有隻死老鼠。
Mitchell 米契爾	Oh, give me a break! Stop complaining! 饒了我吧！別抱怨了！
Mandy 曼蒂	That's easy for you to say. You're not the one that has to sit on a dead rat! Get rid of it! 你說的倒容易。要坐在死老鼠身上的又不是你！幫我處理掉啦！
Mitchell 米契爾	Fine. We'll do as you say. Where is it? 好啦，就照著你的意思做吧！老鼠在哪？

71. can't help　克制不了；沒辦法控制

💬 **真的太好笑了：**

A: Can you stop laughing?
　　你可不可以停止笑啊？

B: I can't help myself.
　　我無法控制我自己。

💬 身不由己：

A: Could you stop *snoring* at night?
你晚上可不可以不要打鼾啊？

B: Sorry, but I can't help it.
對不起，但是我沒辦法控制自己。

💬 無法壓抑：

She can't help crying.
她無法忍住不哭。

* snore	[snor]	動	打鼾

🎧 *Track 079*

72. Nobody knows. / Who knows?
沒人知道（答案）／誰知道？

💬 無法得知：

A: Who did it?
誰做的？

B: Nobody knows.
沒人知道。

💬 到底是誰呀：

A: Who took your book?
誰拿了你的書？

B: Who knows?
誰知道？

Chapter **01** 日常點滴 *Daily Life*

73. **First come, first served.**　先來先招待；捷足先登。

💬 本店不接受訂位：

A: May I make a reservation for tonight?
　　我可以訂今晚的位子嗎？

B: Sorry. We don't take reservations. First come, first served.
　　抱歉，我們不接受訂位，先來先招待！

💬 早一點到，以免客滿：

You had better arrive there early since the restaurant is "first come, first served."
你最好早點到，因為那家餐廳沒有訂位的。

74. **It's not my day!**　今天運氣真糟！

💬 一個不小心：

I *spilled* coffee on my skirt! It's really not my day.
我把咖啡灑到裙子上了！今天真是運氣不好。

💬 天吶，真是沒完沒了：

A: When you finish that report, you have four more to do.
　　當你寫完那份報告，你還有四份要做。

B: It's really not my day!
　　我今天的運氣真糟。

| * spill | [spɪl] | 動 | 使溢流 |

75. **beside the point**　離題的；不是重點

💬 其實還有其他更重要的問題：

A: I hope I will be able to go to the party with you.
　　我希望我能跟你一起參加這個宴會。

B: That is beside the point. What is important now is do you have *suitable* clothes for the party?
　　這不是重點。重點是你有適合的宴會裝嗎？

A: I think we need to buy a bigger house.
　我覺得我們應該要買大一點的房子。

B: That is beside the point. The point is why we need a bigger house.
　這不是重點。重點是為什麼我們需要大一點的房子？

* suit·a·ble	[ˋsutəbl̩]	形	適合的

🎧 *Track 083*

76. hit the jackpot　中大獎；走運

💬 **真令人羨慕啊：**

A: The boss decided to give her a raise today.
　老闆今天決定給她加薪。

B: She hit the jackpot today!
　她今天走運了！

💬 **喔耶：**

I hit the jackpot today! I won $100.
我今天中大獎了！我贏 100 元。

🎧 *Track 084*

77. it's a pain in the neck　很討厭而難避免的傢伙（事情、局面）

💬 **下雨天騎車真的很麻煩：**

It's a pain in the neck riding a motorcycle when it's raining.
在雨天中騎機車很討厭。

💬 **不得不做：**

It's a pain in the neck *sorting* out the letters.
整理信件真的很煩人。

* sort	[sɔrt]	動	分類

Chapter 01 日常點滴 *Daily Life*

78. jump down someone's *throat*
粗暴的回答某人；無理的打斷某人的話

💬 **情有可原：**

A: She had no right to jump down my *throat* like that. I haven't finished talking yet.
她沒權力這麼無理的打斷我的話，我還沒說完！

B: Forgive her. She's had a bad day.
原諒她吧！她今天過得很糟。

💬 **她平常不是這樣的：**

It seems that she was not happy today. She jumped down my *throat* when I asked if she liked my new hairstyle.
她今天似乎不是很開心，當我問她是否喜歡我的新髮型的時候，她凶巴巴的回答我。

* throat	[θrot]	名	喉嚨

79. ...not as good as... 不如……

💬 **修理舊的會比買新的好：**

A: The new washing machine is not as good as the old one.
新的洗衣機不如舊的洗衣機。

B: I told you to fix the old one.
我就叫你去修舊的那一臺吧。

💬 **新的東西未必好：**

A: Why did you throw away the new TV?
你幹嘛把新的電視丟掉？

B: It's not as good as the old one.
它不如老的那一臺。

💬 **比較後才知道：**

The book is not as good as that one.
這本書不如那本書好。

80. save something for a rainy day　以備不時之需

💬 隨時能派上用場：

I think I will save the money for a rainy day.
我想把這錢存起來以備不時之需。

💭 類似的情況：

Don't throw these boxes away. You can save them for a rainy day.
別把這些盒子丟掉，把它們留起來以備不時之需。

😺 Chat 不 斷 流

Jen 珍	It's not my day! 今天運氣真糟！
Paula 寶拉	What happened? 怎麼了？
Jen 珍	Barry just gave me extra work. He is such a pain in the neck! 貝瑞剛才多給我一堆工作，他真的很討厭！
Paula 寶拉	Why did he do that? 他幹嘛這樣對你？
Jen 珍	We were talking about politics, he got upset and jumped down my throat for nothing! 我們剛才在談論政治，我根本沒幹嘛，他就開始生氣，接著無理的打斷我！
Paula 寶拉	He just can't help being a jerk, can he? 他無法克制做出惡劣行徑，對吧？
Jen 珍	Yeah. Honestly, he's not as good as our old manager. 對啊，老實說，之前的經理比他好。
Paula 寶拉	Tell me about it! 那還用說。

Chapter 01 日常點滴 Daily Life

| Jen
珍 | I better save some money for a rainy day. Just in case I wanna quit this job!
我最好多存些錢以備不時之需，免得我哪天想辭職！ |

🎧 *Track 089*

81. give it a try　試試看

💬 要吃吃看我的手藝嗎：

A: I have some cookies. Do you want to give it a try?
　　我有一些餅乾。你要試吃看看嗎？

B: Yes, please.
　　好，謝謝！

💬 再接再勵：

A: Why don't you give it a try one more time?
　　你何不再試一次呢？

B: No, I have had enough.
　　不，我已經試夠了。

💬 加油給動力：

I think you should give it a try.
我覺得你應該試試看。

🎧 *Track 090*

82. get away from it all　遠離這一切

💬 休息是為了走更遠的路：

A: Sometimes I really want to get away from it all.
　　有時候我真想遠離這一切！

B: You are just worn out. You need a vacation!
　　你只是太累了，你需要一個假期！

💬 **拋開一切，重新開始：**

I can't stand my job anymore. I am getting away from it all and start a new life.
我再也受不了我的工作了，我要離開這一切，並重新展開新生活。

🎧 *Track 091*

83. There is no place like home.　沒有比家更溫暖的地方。

💬 **金窩銀窩不如自己的狗窩：**

A: It feels so good to be home.
回到家的感覺真好。

B: Yup, there is no place like home.
是啊，沒有比家更溫暖的地方！

💬 **家是永遠的避風港：**

There is no place like home. It is always safe and warm.
沒有比家更溫暖的地方了，這裡總是既安全又溫暖。

🎧 *Track 092*

84. relax　放輕鬆

💬 **不要把自己逼太緊了：**

A: Hey! I think you need to relax.
喂！我覺得你需要放輕鬆。

B: No, I still have a lot of work to do.
不，我還有許多事要做。

💬 **放寬心吧：**

A: Relax. There is no need to worry.
放輕鬆！不用擔心。

B: Are you sure?
你確定嗎？

💬 **精神別太緊繃：**

Try to relax when you are stressed.
當你壓力大的時候嘗試著放輕鬆。

85. **Don't cry over spilt milk.** 覆水難收。

💬 記性真差：

A: How could I have left my umbrella on the bus?
我怎麼會把我的雨傘留在公車上？

B: Don't cry over spilt milk. Go get a new one.
覆水難收，再買一個新的吧！

💬 一切為時已晚：

A: I was such an idiot. I treated Eileen so badly.
我真是一個大白痴！我以前對艾琳真壞！

B: Don't cry over spilt milk! She is happily married now.
覆水難收！她現在婚姻很幸福。

86. **It wouldn't hurt to ask.** 問人又不會怎樣。

💬 路長在嘴巴上：

A: We are lost again.
我們又迷路了！

B: Let's go ask somebody. It wouldn't hurt to ask.
我們去問人吧！問人又不會少一塊肉。

💬 為什麼不開口問呢：

A: Where is the sugar? I have been looking for it all morning.
糖在哪裡？我一個早上都在找它。

B: You should have asked earlier. It wouldn't hurt to ask.
你應該早一點問啊！問人又不會少一塊肉。

87. **You can be at ease.** 你放一百二十個心！

💬 拍胸脯保證：

A: Leave everything to me. You can be at ease.
把一切都交給我吧！你放一百二十個心！

B: Are you sure?
你確定嗎？

A: You can be at ease. Peter is here to help you.
你放一百二十個心！彼特會幫你的。

B: Thank God.
感謝天。

🎧 *Track 096*

88. I've changed my mind. 我改變心意了。

○ **改變想法：**

A: I thought you were coming.
我以為妳會來。

B: I've changed my mind.
我改變心意了。

○ **同樣的意思：**

A: Didn't you want this watch?
妳不是要這隻錶嗎？

B: I've changed my mind.
我改變心意了。

○ **也可以這樣說：**

I've changed my mind, so I won't go with you.
我改變心意了，所以我不會跟你去。

🎧 *Track 097*

89. have one's head in the clouds 心不在焉

○ **分心了：**

A: Hey! Are you listening to me?
喂！你在聽我說話嗎？

B: I am sorry. I had my head in the clouds.
對不起，我剛剛心不在焉。

○ **凡事不專心，難有好結果：**

A: Joe always has his head in the clouds in class.
喬上課時總是心不在焉的。

B: No wonder his grades are really bad.
難怪他的成績很糟糕。

Chapter 01 日常點滴 *Daily Life*

90. I'm off (to...)　我要去……

💬 **去哪裡啊：**

A: Where are you going?
　　你要去哪裡？

B: I am off to the bank.
　　我要去銀行。

💬 **要不要順便幫你買什麼東西：**

A: I am off to the market. Do you need anything?
　　我要去市場，你需要什麼嗎？

B: No, thank you.
　　不了，謝謝。

💬 **直接表明目的地：**

I'm off to the department store.
我要去百貨公司。

🐱 Chat 不斷流

Alex 艾莉絲	I feel so lonely in this city. I just want to get away from it all. 這座城市讓我感到很孤獨，我只想遠離這一切。
Piper 派佩	I know how you feel. There is no place like home. 我懂你的感受，沒有比家更溫暖的地方。
Alex 艾莉絲	I've had my head in the clouds at work. I've changed my mind. I want to switch career paths. 我最近上班都心不在焉，我改變心意了，我想轉換跑道。
Piper 派佩	Really? What do you want to do instead? 真的？你想改做什麼？
Alex 艾莉絲	I want to be a philosopher. 我想當哲學家。

Piper 派佩	Interesting choice! I happen to have a friend that teaches philosophy at university. Do you want me to ask her for you? 很有趣的選擇，我剛好認識朋友在大學教哲學，要我幫你問問她嗎？
Alex 艾莉絲	Nah. It's fine. I'll think of something myself. 不了，沒關係，我會自己想辦法。
Piper 派佩	Oh, it wouldn't hurt to ask! 噢，問問又不會怎樣！

🎧 *Track 100*

91. turn over a new leaf　重新開始

💬 **一切歸零，重新出發：**

You should turn over a new leaf from the beginning of next year.
你應該在明年初的時候重新開始。

💬 **痛改前非：**

I used to smoke, but I turned over a new leaf when I got a lung disease.
我以前抽菸，但自從我的肺生病了以後，我就改過自新了。

🎧 *Track 101*

92. Something is better than nothing.　有總比沒有好。

💬 **聊勝於無：**

A: Can you believe it? Mother's Day freebies from this department store are only those table settings.
你相信嗎？這家百貨公司在母親節送的贈品只有碗筷類的東西。

B: Well, something is better than nothing.
哎呀！有總比沒有好吧？

💬 **只能退而求其次：**

A: There is only milk left in the refrigerator.
冰箱裡只剩下牛奶了。

B: Something is better than nothing. I am *starving*.
有東西吃總比沒東西吃好，我快餓死了。

| * starve | [starv] | 動 | 餓死、饑餓 |

🎧 *Track 102*

93. The early bird catches the worm.　早起的鳥兒有蟲吃。

💬 **早起的人比較容易成功：**

A: What do you get up so early for?
你幹嘛這麼早起？

B: Don't you know that the early bird catches the worm?
你不知道嗎？早起的鳥兒有蟲吃。

💭 **早睡早起好處多：**

Don't sleep in; the early bird catches the worm.
別睡懶覺；早起的鳥兒有蟲吃。

🎧 *Track 103*

94. Tomorrow is another day.　明天又是嶄新的一天。

💬 **養精蓄銳，蓄勢待發：**

A: I feel so tired.
我好累喔！

B: Go to bed. Tomorrow is another day.
去睡一覺，明天又是嶄新的一天。

💭 **人要向前看：**

A: Nothing went right today.
今天諸事不順。

B: Don't worry. Tomorrow will be another day.
別擔心，明天又是嶄新的一天。

🎧 *Track 104*

95. bury the hatchet　言歸於好；和好

💬 **盡釋前嫌，和好如初：**

A: Could we please make up? I miss you so much.
我們可以和好嗎？我好想你。

B: Yes, let's bury the hatchet.
可以的。讓我們和好吧！

➳ 仇人變朋友：

A: I thought they were enemies.
　　我以為他們是仇人。

B: They used to be, but they decide to bury the hatchet and become friends.
　　他們以前是，但他們已經重新開始成為朋友了。

🎧 *Track 105*

96. pay through the nose　花很多錢

➳ 一分錢一分貨：

A: You will have to pay through the nose when you go to that restaurant.
　　你去那家飯店要花很多錢。

B: Is the charge of the restaurant that expensive?
　　有那麼貴嗎？

➳ 所費不貲：

We paid through the nose for that sofa.
買那張沙發真是花了我們一大筆錢。

🎧 *Track 106*

97. What's done is done.　做了就做了。

➳ 已成定局了：

A: We paid too much for the rent.
　　我們付太多房租錢了。

B: What's done is done. You have already signed the contract.
　　事情已成事實了，你已經簽了合約了。

➳ 一言既出，駟馬難追：

A: I really *regret* helping her out as the treasurer.
　　我很後悔答應她當總務。

B: What's done is done. Just do your best.
　　事情做都做了，你就盡力吧！

* re·gret	[rɪˋgrɛt]	動	後悔、遺憾

Chapter 01 日常點滴 *Daily Life*

98. **Variety is the spice of life.** 多樣化豐富生活。

💭 **生活不能一成不變：**

A: I haven't seen a movie for a long time.
我好久沒看過電影了。

B: You should go see one. Variety is the spice of life.
你應該去看一部的。變化使生活豐富。

💭 **改變習慣，改變運命：**

A: I have been watching TV all afternoon.
我整個下午都在看電視。

B: Variety is the spice of life. You should form a new habit.
多樣化豐富生活，你應該培養一個新的習慣。

99. **In other words,...** 換句話說

💭 **相同的意思換個說法：**

A: I like cold weather.
我喜歡冷的天氣。

B: In other words, you like winter.
換句話說，你喜歡冬天。

💭 **也可以這樣說：**

A: I like farm animals.
我喜歡農場的動物。

B: In other words, you like cows and pigs.
換句話說，你喜歡牛和豬。

💭 **言下之意：**

In other words, you don't like the restaurant.
換句話說，你不喜歡這家餐廳。

100. *Haste* makes waste.　欲速則不達。

💬 吃快弄破碗：

A: I was rushing to go out and left my cell phone in the kitchen.
　　我剛剛急著出門，把手機忘在廚房了。

B: *Haste* makes waste.
　　欲速則不達。

💬 樂極生悲，得不償失：

A: He was hurrying to join a wedding but got into a car accident on the way.
　　他急著去參加一個婚禮，卻在途中發生車禍。

B: *Haste* makes waste.
　　欲速則不達。

* haste	[hest]	名	急忙、急速

😺 Chat 不 斷 流

Gus 葛斯	I thought Freddy and I finally buried the hatchet after all these years. 我還以為這麼多年後，佛萊迪終於要跟我和好了。
Vincent 文森	But you didn't? 你們沒有和好嗎？
Gus 葛斯	No, not at all! 不，才沒有！
Vincent 文森	What happened? 發生什麼事？
Gus 葛斯	He broke my ribs just because I ate his chocolate chip cookies! 我只是吃了他的巧克力碎片餅乾，他就把我的肋骨打斷！

Chapter 01 日常點滴 Daily Life

Vincent 文森	Oh, wow. That's extreme. 天啊，他的手段真激烈。
Gus 葛斯	I paid through the nose for my medical bills! 害我花了很多醫療費！
Vincent 文森	I hope he's going to turn over a new leaf someday. 我希望他有一天能改過自新。
Gus 葛斯	In other words, you hope Freddy can finally stop being a moron. 換句話說，你希望佛萊迪有天不再當個蠢蛋。
Vincent 文森	Get some rest, tomorrow is another day. 去休息吧，明天又是嶄新的一天。

🎧 *Track 111*

101. like a bull in a china shop　笨手笨腳；莽撞行事

💬 越忙越要放輕鬆：

A: I felt like a bull in a china shop on my brother's wedding.
　　在我哥哥的婚禮時，我覺得自己笨手笨腳的。

B: That's because you were too nervous.
　　那是因為你太緊張了。

💬 越幫越忙：

When my brother helps my mom with the work in the kitchen,
he is always like a bull in a china shop.
當我哥哥在廚房裡幫媽媽忙時，他總是笨手笨腳的。

🎧 *Track 112*

102. I don't have a *clue*.　我不知道。

💬 無法預知狀況：

A: Do you know if it's going to rain tomorrow?
　　你知不知道明天會不會下雨？

B: I don't have a *clue*.
　　我不知道！

💬 **一頭霧水：**

A: What happened to Joey's parrot?
喬伊的鸚鵡怎麼了？

B: I don't have a *clue*. I don't even know that he's got a bird.
我不知道。我還不知道他有一隻鳥呢！

* clue	[klu]	名	線索

🎧 *Track 113*

103. Better safe than sorry.　寧願安全（可靠）也不要後悔。

💬 **做事保險一點的好：**

A: It's not raining outside. I don't want to bring an umbrella.
外面沒下雨，我不想帶雨傘了。

B: Take it with you. Better safe than sorry.
帶著吧！帶著可靠點。

💬 **安全至上：**

Drive slowly. Better safe than sorry.
開慢一點，寧願安全也不要後悔。

🎧 *Track 114*

104. for crying out loud　（加強語氣）哎呀呀！拜託！

💬 **可以不要再想了嗎：**

A: Where is my money? What am I supposed to do?
我的錢跑哪去？我該怎麼辦？

B: For crying out loud, stop worrying about money.
天啊！請你別再擔心錢的事了！

💬 **拜託你好不好：**

Please be quiet for crying out loud.
我拜託你安靜一點。

Chapter 01 日常點滴 Daily Life

105. on the *spur* of the moment 一時衝動；一時興起

💬 **突如其來的行為：**

She ran up to the stage and sang on the *spur* of the moment.
她一時興起跑上台去唱歌。

💬 **突發其想的決定：**

On the *spur* of the moment, Matthew decided to quit his job and go traveling around the world.
馬修一時衝動，決定辭去他的工作並去環遊世界。

* spur	[spɜ]	名	刺激物

106. Every little bit counts. 一點一滴都算。

💬 **積沙成塔：**

A: Are you depositing $100?
你要存 100 塊啊？

B: Why not? Every little bit counts.
為什麼不？一點一滴都算啊！

💬 **滴水都能滙成河：**

A: I have studied so hard for the test, and it has finally paid off.
我為了那考試很努力的讀書，終於有了代價了。

B: I know. Every little bit counts.
我知道，一點一滴都算。

107. in the same boat 面臨相同的事；相同的命運（同病相憐）

💬 **同是天涯淪落人：**

A: Could you lend me some money to pay for the rent?
你可不可以借我一些錢來付租金？

B: I am in the same boat with you. I could hardly pay mine.
我和你的處境一樣，我自己的都快付不起了。

二人同心，其力斷金：

We are in the same boat here, so let's face it together.
我們現在同病相憐，所以讓我們一起面對它吧。

🎧 *Track 118*

108. **Money doesn't grow on trees.**　金錢得來不易。

天下沒有白吃的午餐：

A: Dad, can you raise my allowance?
　　爸爸，你可不可多給我一點零用錢？

B: Money doesn't grow on trees. You have to earn them yourself.
　　金錢得來不易，你得自己去賺！

世上沒有不勞而獲的事：

A: I want to buy this diamond ring.
　　我要買個鑽石戒指！

B: I don't have that much money. Money doesn't grow on trees.
　　You know?
　　我沒那麼多錢，你知道錢不是長在樹上的吧！

🎧 *Track 119*

109. **It's on me.**　我來付。

我請你喝酒：

A: The beer is on me.
　　啤酒我請。

B: Thank you.
　　謝謝。

這麼大方，要下紅雨了：

A: Dinner is on me.
　　晚餐算我的。

B: When did you become so *generous*?
　　你什麼時候變得那麼大方？

* gen·er·ous	[ˈdʒɛnərəs]		慷慨的、大方的

110. **Boys will be boys.**　男生就是男生。

💬 **本性難移：**

A: My son came in with ***mud*** all over him.
我兒子回來一身都是泥。

B: Boys will be boys.
男生就是男生。

💬 **男人總是大而化之：**

A: It was so inconsiderate of him to leave me there alone.
他讓我一個人在那裡等，真是不體貼。

B: Boys will be boys.
男生就是男生。

* mud	[mʌd]	名	爛泥

👩‍🦰 Chat 不 斷 流

Linda 琳達	Jeez! You spilled wine on my skirt! 老天，你把紅酒灑在我的裙子上了！
Waitress 服務生	I'm terribly sorry. I'll pay for the dry-cleaning! Sorry about that! 非常抱歉，我會付乾洗費的，真的很對不起！
Linda 琳達	Oh wow. That waitress is like a bull in a china shop! 天啊，那位服務生真的是笨手笨腳！
Bob 巴布	Maybe she is a newbie. 也許她是新來的。
Linda 琳達	I don't have a clue, but she sure is clumsy. 我不知道，但她確實很笨拙。
Bob 巴布	This meal is on me. 這餐我請。

Linda 琳達	Oh come on, let's at least split the bills. Money doesn't grow on trees. 別這樣，至少讓我出一半吧，金錢可得來不易。
Bob 巴布	No, I insist. 不，我堅持要請。
Linda 琳達	Ugh, boys will be boys! 噢，男生就是男生。

111.It's never too late to learn.
學習永遠不嫌晚；亡羊補牢猶未晚。

💬 改變從現在開始：

A: I really want to learn to play the flute although I am already 35.
雖然我已經 35 歲了，但是我真的很想學笛子。

B: It's never too late to learn.
學習永遠不嫌晚。

💬 只要開始就是好事：

I know I am a little old for learning tap dancing, but it's never too late to learn.
我知道我現在開始學踢踏舞有點晚了，但是學習永遠不嫌晚。

Chapter 01 日常點滴 *Daily Life*

112. What you see is what you get.
你看到什麼（東西、物品）就是什麼。

💬 **只有這些選擇而已：**

A: Are there any other colors?
有沒有其它的顏色？

B: No, I am sorry. What you see is what you get.
沒有，對不起，有的就是你看到的這些了。

💬 **不能再少了：**

A: If you could lower the price, I will buy it.
如果你把價錢降低一點，我就買了！

B: I am sorry I can't lower the price anymore. What you see is what you get.
對不起，我不能再降了，就是你看到的這個價錢了。

113. zero in on something　專注於……；對準

💬 **對準目標下手：**

A: What shall we buy at the supermarket?
我們應該到超市買些什麼？

B: Because we don't have too much money left, we'd better zero in on just some daily necessities.
因為我們錢所剩的不多，我們最好專買一些日常用品。

💬 **集中精神，專心一致：**

You should zero in on programming.
你應該將注意力放在程式設計上。

114. by the book　按照規定

💬 **按表操課的執行：**

A: What shall we do to make this project more *practical*?
我們應該怎麼做來讓這個計畫更可行？

B: Let's finish this project by the book first.
我們把這計畫先按照規定做完。

💬 **必須要這樣的：**

You have to do everything by the book in this company.
在這間公司你必須照規定行事。

* prac·ti·cal	[ˈpræktɪkl]	形	實用的

🎧 *Track 126*

115. That's all, folks!　就這樣囉，各位！

💬 **那就先這樣囉：**

A: That's all, folks! See you next time!
　　就這樣囉，各位！下次再見！

B: See you.
　　再見！

💬 **到此告一段落：**

That's all, folks! It's time to go home.
就這樣囉，各位！該回家了。

🎧 *Track 127*

116. feel something in one's bones　（某人）的直覺

💬 **憑感覺臆測：**

A: How do you know it is going to rain tomorrow?
　　你怎麼知道明天會下雨？

B: I can feel it in my bones.
　　我的直覺啊！

💬 **天生的第六感：**

A How do you know something big is going to happen
　　tomorrow?
　　你怎麼知道明天會有大事發生？

B: I don't know, but I can feel it in my bones.
　　我不知道，但是我直覺告訴我的！

Chapter 01 日常點滴 Daily Life

117. **Mother knows best.**　媽媽最知道了。

💬 **還是媽媽最懂我：**

A: My mother really knows me.
　　我媽媽真的很了解我。

B: Well, they say mother knows best.
　　他們說，媽媽最清楚自己的小孩囉！

💬 **果然媽媽最了解：**

A: My mother suggested that I study French literature.
　　我媽媽建議我去學法國文學。

B: Mother knows best. You have always liked literature.
　　媽媽最清楚了，你一直都很喜歡文學。

118. **Out of the question!**　不可能的！

💬 **門兒都沒有：**

A: Could I borrow your bike?
　　我可以借你的單車嗎？

B: Out of the question!
　　不可能！

💬 **否定的答案：**

A: Do you think John dumped Mary?
　　你覺得是約翰把瑪麗甩了嗎？

B: Out of the question! He loves her very much.
　　不可能的！他很愛她。

119. **I can't imagine.**　我不能想像。

💬 **令人無法相信：**

A: The apples were bigger than my hand.
　　那些蘋果比我的手大。

B: I can't imagine.
　　我不能想像。

不可思議：

A: The horse runs faster than the car.
那匹馬跑得比車快。

B: I can't imagine.
我不能想像。

真的假的：

I can't imagine that she is pregnant.
我無法想像她懷孕了。

🎧 *Track 131*

120. It's hard to say.　很難說。

不一定：

A: Will he be late?
他會遲到嗎？

B: It's hard to say.
很難說。

還沒決定：

A: Will you go?
你會去嗎？

B: It's hard to say.
很難說。

無法確切地說明：

It's hard to say whether I like it or not.
很難說我到底喜不喜歡。

Chapter 01 日常點滴 *Daily Life*

🐾 Chat 不斷流

John 約翰	Where is Kevin? 凱文呢？
Mary 瑪莉	I don't know. He might be at the playground. 不知道，可能在操場吧。
John 約翰	But I told him to stay here! 但我叫他待在這裡！
Mary 瑪莉	Well, he never does things by the book. Why do you think he will listen to you this time? 他從來不守規矩，你怎麼認為他這次會聽你的？
John 約翰	Maybe he's been kidnapped! I just feel it in my bones! 也許他被綁架了，我有這樣的預感。
Mary 瑪莉	I can't imagine. 我不能想像。
John 約翰	It's hard to say. 這很難説。
Mary 瑪莉	Look! That's Kevin right there! 看，凱文就在那！
John 約翰	Oh right, mothers know best. 好吧，媽媽最知道了。

121. Forgive and forget.　不念舊惡。

💬 **寬容以待：**

A: She acted like nothing happened, and she gave me such an attitude!
她一副若無其事的樣子，而且態度糟得很。

B: Oh, come on, forgive and forget!
算了吧！

💭 **做人有容乃大：**

He didn't mean to hurt you, forgive and forget!
他不是故意傷害你的，算了吧！

🎧 *Track 134*

122. **Those were the days.** 那真是好時光。

💬 **我曾經的少女時代：**

A: We were young and pretty, weren't we?
我們當時既年輕又漂亮，不是嗎？

B: Those were the days.
那真是好時光！

💭 **記得當時年紀小：**

A: Remember we used to go fishing in that lake when we were kids?
還記不記得我們以前小時候常到那個湖邊去釣魚？

B: Yeah, those were the days. Now the lake is *polluted*.
是啊，那真是好時光，現在湖水都被污染了。

* pol·lute	[pə`lut]	動	污染

🎧 *Track 135*

123. **There is a time and a place for everything.**
在適合的時候派上用場；適時做事。

💬 **總有用武之地：**

A: Why do I have to learn English?
我為什麼要讀英文？

B: There is a time and a place for everything.
因為總是會在適合的時候派上用場的。

💭 **凡事要因時因地制宜：**

A: Have I ever showed you the scar on my belly?
我有沒有給你看過我肚子上的疤？

B: There is a time and a place for everything, but here in the middle of the street is inappropriate.
做事要看場合和時間，現在在馬路中間並不適合吧！

Chapter 01 日常點滴 *Daily Life*

124. **You can't win them all.**
人不可能一直走運；人不可能事事都一帆風順。

💬 <u>花無百日紅，人無千日好：</u>

A: I can't believe that I lost the game to them.
我真不敢相信我竟然輸給了他們！

B: You can't win them all! You will do better next time.
人不可能一直走運，你下一次會做得更好的！

💬 **知足方能常樂：**

A: I have a great family and a great job, but I am still not
satisfied.
我有一個很棒的家庭、一份很好的工作，但是我還是不滿足。

B: You can't win them all.
你不可能什麼事都一帆風順的！

* sat·is·fy	[ˈsætɪsˌfaɪ]	動	使滿足

125. **give something one's best shot**　盡最大的努力

💬 **即使沒有把握，也要全力以赴：**

A: It sounds difficult to pass this exam.
要通過這個考試似乎很難。

B: All you can do is give it your best shot.
你所能做的就是盡你最大的努力。

💬 **竭盡所能：**

I don't know if I could pass the exam, but I will give it my best
shot.
我不知道我會不會通過這考試，但我會盡我最大的努力的。

126. If you can't stand the *heat*, get out of the kitchen.
受不了（壓力），就離開吧。

💭 **沒辦法再繼續下去：**

A: I can't stand my work anymore.
我再也沒辦法忍受我的工作了！

B: If you can't stand the *heat*, get out of the kitchen.
你若是受不了壓力，就離開吧！

💭 **道不同，不相為謀：**

A: Those people down at the club are such snobs.
那些在俱樂部的人都是一些自大的傢伙。

B: If you can't stand the *heat*, get out of the kitchen.
你若是受不了，就離開吧！

* heat	[hit]	名	熱、熱度

127. Don't spend it all in one place. 不要全部花在同一個地方。

💭 **花錢容易賺錢難：**

A: I am going to spend all my salary on clothes.
我要把我所有的薪水花在買衣服上。

B: Don't spend it all in one place.
不要全部花在同一個地方。

💭 **中了一筆意外之財：**

A: I won $10000!
我贏了一萬元。

B: Great! But don't spend it all in one place.
很好，但是不要全部花在同一個地方。

Chapter 01 日常點滴 *Daily Life*

128. There is no time like the present.
沒有比現在更適合的時候了。

💬 **就是現在：**

A: When can I talk you alone?
我什麼時候可以跟你單獨說話？

B: There is no time like the present.
沒有比現在更適合的時候了。

💬 **打鐵要趁熱：**

A: We will have to make a plan for our vacation.
我必須為我們的假期做一個計畫。

B: There is no time like the present. Let's talk about it now.
沒有比現在更適合的時候了，我們現在就來談談吧！

129. It's not *worth* it.　不值得。

💬 **真是浪費：**

A: I spent two thousand dollars on this teapot.
我花了兩千元買這茶壺。

B: It's not *worth* it.
不值得。

💬 **不要花冤枉錢了：**

A: Should I buy this watch?
我該買這支錶嗎？

B: No, it's not *worth* it.
不，不值得。

* worth	[wɜθ]	形	值得的

130. Allow me. 讓我來。

💬 **太重了，我搬不動：**

A: This box is so heavy.
　　這盒子好重。

B: Then allow me.
　　讓我來吧！

💬 **我來幫忙：**

A: Please allow me to open the door for you.
　　讓我來幫你開門。

B: Thank you.
　　謝謝。

💬 **伸出援手：**

Allow me to help you.
讓我來幫你。

👾 **Chat 不 斷 流**

Ken 肯恩	Do you remember how Dave used to pick on me when we were younger? 你記得我們年輕時，大衛總是欺負我嗎？
Dale 戴爾	Oh yeah. Those were the days. 記得啊，那真是有趣的一段歲月。
Ken 肯恩	Guess what? My company just hired him. I'm his supervisor now! I will give it my best shot to make his life miserable. 你猜怎麼著？我們公司最近僱用他，現在我是他主管。我會盡最大的努力，讓他的人生變得很悲慘。
Dale 戴爾	You know there is a time and a place for everything. 你懂做事要看時機、地點吧？

Chapter 01 日常點滴 *Daily Life*

Ken 肯恩	There is no time like the present. 沒有比現在更適合的時候了
Dale 戴爾	Don't do that. It's not even worth it! 別這樣，這根本不值得！
Ken 肯恩	Well I mean, if you can't stand the heat, get out of the kitchen. 如果他受不了壓力，就離開吧。
Dale 戴爾	You should forgive and forget. Move on! 你該不念舊惡，放下吧。

🎧 *Track 144*

131. Take a seat. / Be seated.　請坐。

💬 請稍等一下：

A: Please take a seat, Mr. Wang will be right with you.
請坐，王先生馬上來了。

B: Thank you.
謝謝。

💬 你可以坐著等：

Take a seat first and I'll come back to you later.
請先坐下，我等等就回來找你。

💬 要上課了：

Please be seated. The teacher is coming.
請坐下，老師要來了。

🎧 *Track 145*

132. Go ahead.　請便。

💬 無妨的：

A: Excuse me, I want to go to the bathroom.
對不起，我要去上個廁所。

B: Go ahead.
你請便吧！

我一點都不介意：

A: Do you mind if I use your car?
你介不介意我用你的車？

B: Go ahead.
你請便吧！

🎧 *Track 146*

133. hardly have time to breathe　沒有喘息的時間

忙得手都沒有停過：

A: You look so tired today.
你今天看起來好累喔！

B: I have been working all day and hardly have time to breathe.
我今天做了一天的事，我幾乎沒有休息的時間呢！

讓我喘口氣吧：

I hardly had time to breathe today. Please give me a break.
我今天幾乎沒有喘息的時間！請讓我休息一下吧！

* breathe	[briθ]	動	呼吸、生存

🎧 *Track 147*

134. Keep your eye on the ball.　專心。

比賽不要分心：

A: Hey, what do you want to do tonight?
喂！你今天晚上想做什麼？

B: Keep your eye on the ball. We'll talk about it after the game.
你專心一點！比賽完再說吧！

集中注意力：

Keep your eye on the ball. Don't miss another ball!
你專心一點，別再漏接球了！

Chapter 01 日常點滴 *Daily Life*

135. leave no stone unturned　徹底；不遺餘力

💬 到處都翻遍了：

A: Have you looked everywhere?
　　你到處都找了嗎？

B: Yes, I have left no stone unturned, but I still can't find my watch.
　　有啊！我到處都找了，可是就是找不到我的手錶。

💬 不達目的絕不罷休：

Leave no stone unturned until the missing child is found.
徹底的搜查，直到失蹤的小孩找到為止！

136. I'll do my best.　我盡量；我盡力。

💬 卯足全力：

A: Please help me.
　　請救我。

B: I'll do my best.
　　我盡力。

💬 一定幫忙：

A: Please ask her for me.
　　請幫我問問看她。

B: I'll do my best.
　　我盡量。

💬 亡羊補牢，為時不晚：

I'll do my best to *solve* the problem.
我盡力解決問題。

* solve	[salv]	動	解決

137. **I mean it.** 我是說真的。

💬 很嚴肅地的告知：

A: Do I have to do the laundry today?
　　我今天一定要洗衣服嗎？

B: Yes, you have to, and I mean it.
　　是的，你必須今天洗，而且我是說真的。

💭 我不是在開玩笑：

Stop that! I mean it.
住手，我是說真的。

138. **The end justifies the means.** 為目的不擇手段。

💬 劫富濟貧，行俠仗義：

A: Robinhood stole from the rich and helped the poor.
　　羅賓漢偷有錢人的錢去幫助窮人。

B: The end justifies the means.
　　只要目的正當，就可以不擇手段。

💭 有時需要善意的謊言：

A: I tricked her into having a health checkup.
　　我把她騙去做了一個身體檢查。

B: In that case, the end justifies the means.
　　這麼來說的話，你意圖對了，手段就不重要了。

* jus·ti·fy	[ˈdʒʌstəˌfaɪ]	動	證明……有理

139. Life's full of surprises. 人生充滿了驚喜。

💬 無法置信：

A: Are you getting married? I can't believe it!
你要結婚了？我真不敢相信！

B: Yup! Life's full of surprises.
是啊！人生是充滿了驚喜！

💬 也太巧合了吧：

A: Wow! What a surprise to see you here.
在這裡遇見你真是驚訝！

B: Life's full of surprises.
人生是充滿了驚喜！

140. Fancy meeting you here! 怎麼會在這裡遇見你！

💬 地球是圓的：

A: Sarah! Fancy meeting you here!
莎拉！怎麼會在這裡遇見妳啊！

B: We haven't seen each other for such a long time.
我們好久沒見到對方了。

💬 出乎意料之外：

A: John, fancy meeting you here!
約翰！怎會在這裡遇見你啊！

B: I thought you didn't like rock'n'roll.
我以為你不喜歡搖滾樂。

* fan·cy	['fænsɪ]	名	愛好

141. You're out of your mind! / You've got to be out of your mind! 你瘋囉！

💬 當有人口出狂言：

A: Let's jump down from here.
我們從這裡跳下去。

B: You've got to be out of your mind!
你一定是瘋了！

💬 同樣的表達：

You're out of your mind! It's impossible.
你瘋囉！這根本不可能。

142. come in handy 派得上用場

💬 未雨綢繆：

I will buy this hammer. You never know when it will come in handy.
我要買這個榔頭，你不會知道它何時可以派得上用場呢！

💬 以備不時之需：

Let's keep this flashlight. It might come in handy someday.
我們把這個手電筒留下吧！它有一天也許會派得上用場。

Chapter 01 日常點滴 *Daily Life*

🐱Chat 不斷流

Bruno 布魯諾	Alain, go ahead and be seated.
	阿倫,來,請坐吧。

Alain 阿倫	Thank you. What's going on?
	謝謝,找我什麼事?

Bruno 布魯諾	You know we have an upcoming project, right?
	你知道我們接下來有項新計畫,對吧?

Alain 阿倫	Yes, I am aware.
	是的,我知道。

Bruno 布魯諾	I want you to keep your eye on the ball and do whatever it takes to achieve our goal.
	我要你專心進行這項計畫,不計一切地達成我們的目標。

Alain 阿倫	You're out of your mind!
	你瘋囉!

Bruno 布魯諾	I mean it. The end justifies the means.
	我是說真的,為目的不擇手段。

Alain 阿倫	Alright, I'll do my best. I will leave no stone unturned.
	好吧,我會盡力,不遺餘力地完成這項計畫。

Chapter 2

- 人際社交 -

Interpersonal Relationships

Chapter 02 音檔雲端連結

因各家手機系統不同，若無法直接掃描，
仍可以至以下電腦雲端連結下載收聽。
（https://tinyurl.com/3e8bz8dy）

🦜 Chat 聊不停

🎧 *Track 157*

01. Keep it up! 繼續努力；繼續加油！

💬 **做得很好，肯定鼓勵：**

You are doing a good job. Keep it up!
你做得很好！請繼續努力（保持下去）！

💭 **可以更好，支持打氣：**

Sally, you have *improved* a lot. Keep it up!
莎莉，你進步了很多，請繼續加油！

* im·prove	[ɪmˋpruv]	動	改善、促進

🎧 *Track 158*

02. Nice to meet you. 幸會、幸會。

💬 **百聞不如一見：**

A: This is my little sister, Karen.
　　這是我妹妹，凱倫。

B: Nice to meet you. I have heard a lot about you from your sister.
　　幸會，幸會！我常聽你姐姐提起你。

💭 **初次見面，高興相識：**

A: Nice to meet you!
　　幸會，幸會。

B: My *pleasure*.
　　這是我的榮幸。

* plea·sure	[ˋplɛʒɚ]	名	愉悅

03. **I don't mind.** 我不介意。

💬 慷慨應允別人要求：

A: Do you mind letting me use your car on the weekend?
你介不介意我週末用你的車？

B: No, I don't mind.
不，我不介意。

💬 回應別人禮貌性地詢問：

A: Do you mind if I smoke here?
你介不介意我在這裡抽菸？

B: No, I don't mind.
不，我不介意。

* smoke	[smok]	動	抽菸

04. **Good job! / Great job! / Nice going!** 幹得好！

💬 稱讚別人表現優異：

A: I got 100 in math!
我數學考一百分。

B: Good job!
做得好！

💬 贊同他人的做法：

A: I told her to mind her own *business*.
我叫她別多管閒事。

B: Nice going! I am fed up with her myself.
幹的好！我自己也受不了她了。

💬 讚揚別人還可以這麼說：

Good job! You are great.
做的好，你真棒。

* busi·ness	['bɪznɪs]	名	商業、買賣

05. May I help you? / What's up?　我可以幫你嗎？／有事嗎？

💬 別人需要幫助：

A: May I help you?
我可以幫你嗎？

B: Yes, I am looking for Dr. Lee.
是的，我在找李醫師。

💭 關心詢問：

A: Hey! What's up?
喂！有事嗎？

B: Nothing much.
沒什麼。

06. I can't promise.　我不敢保證。

💬 別人提出要求時，無法輕易允諾：

A: I need you to finish this tonight.
我要你今晚把這個完成。

B: I can't promise.
我不敢保證。

💭 對事情的不確定：

A: I can't promise that I'll come tomorrow.
我不敢保證明天會來。

B: Why?
為什麼？

07. What are you up to lately?　最近忙些什麼呢？

💬 好久不見，問候近況：

A: What are you up to lately?
最近忙些什麼呢？

B: The same things.
同樣的事情啊。

關心近期動態：

A: What are you up to lately?
最近忙些什麼呢？

B: I am studying for my finals.
我在準備期末考試。

🎧 *Track 164*

08. **What time is it?　幾點了？**

問時間：

A: What time is it?
現在幾點了？

B: It's time for you to go to bed.
該是你睡覺的時間了。

抱怨不守時：

A: Wendy is always late. What time is it?
溫蒂每一次都遲到，現在幾點了？

B: It's already five.
現在已經五點了。

🎧 *Track 165*

09. **What date is today?　今天是幾號？**

問日期：

A: What date is today?
今天是幾號？

B: It's the fifth.
今天是五號。

別人準確地回答：

A: What date is today?
今天是幾號？

B: It's the first.
今天是一號。

10. Time flies. 時間飛逝。

💬 **感嘆光陰似箭：**

It's been ten years since I last saw you. Time really flies.
自從我上次見到你已經十年了，真是時間飛逝啊！

💬 **驚訝時間變遷帶來的轉變：**

I still *remember* when you were a child. Now you're a beautiful young lady. How time flies!
你現在是一個年輕的漂亮女孩了，我還記得你小時候的樣子呢！真是時間飛逝啊！

* re·mem·ber	[rɪˋmɛmbɚ]	動	記得

🧑 Chat 不 斷 流

Jake 傑克	Hey, Kevin! What's up? 嘿，凱文！最近怎麼樣？
Kevin 凱文	Nothing much. What are you up to lately? 沒什麼，你最近忙些什麼呢？
Jake 傑克	I am actually moving tomorrow. 我明天要搬家。
Kevin 凱文	Really? To where? 真的嗎？搬到哪去？
Jake 傑克	I am moving to San Fransisco. 我要搬去舊金山。
Kevin 凱文	Do you need a hand? 需要幫忙嗎？
Jake 傑克	Some help would certainly be nice. 有人幫忙當然好。

Kevin 凱文	What time? It's my sister's birthday tomorrow. 幾點？明天我妹妹生日。
Jake 傑克	4 pm. 下午四點。
Kevin 凱文	I'll try to make it, but I can't promise. 我會盡量去幫你，但我不敢保證。
Jake 傑克	Thanks, Kevin. 謝了，凱文。

🎧 *Track 168*

11. Time is money.　時間就是金錢。

💬 珍惜一分一秒：

A: Why are you in such a *rush*?
你那麼急幹嘛？

B: Don't you know? Time is money.
你不知道嗎？時間就是金錢！

💬 催促對方，抓緊時間：

You better *hurry* up! Time is money.
你得快一點！時間就是金錢！

* hur·ry	['hɝɪ]	動	（使）趕緊
* rush	[rʌʃ]	名	急忙、突進

12. I'm not sure. 我不確定。

💬 **回覆邀約：**

A: Can you come?
你可以來嗎？

B: I'm not sure.
我不確定。

💬 **無法掌握狀況：**

A: Is she here?
她在這裡嗎？

B: I'm not sure.
我不確定。

💬 **拿不定主意：**

I'm not sure if I want to go with you.
我不確定我想不想跟你去。

13. That's because... 那是因為……

💬 **說明原委：**

A: Why did you *leave* your job?
你為什麼離開你的工作？

B: That's because my boss fired me.
那是因為老闆把我開除了。

💬 **事出有因：**

A: Do you know why she is crying?
你知道她為什麼在哭嗎？

B: That's because her mother died.
那是因為她媽媽死了。

* leave	[liv]	動	離開

14. Now you're talking!　這才對嘛！

💬 **表示贊同他人：**

A: OK, OK, I will forget about everything and enjoy tonight.
好啦！好啦！我會忘掉一切，好好享受今晚。

B: Now you're talking! Just relax!
這才對嘛！儘管好好的放鬆一下你自己。

💬 **你很上道：**

A: Fine, I will *lend* you $2000 more.
好，我再多借你 2000 元。

B: Now you're talking!
這才對嘛！

* lend	[lɛnd]	動	借出

15. Whose is it?　這是誰的東西？

💬 **尋找失主：**

A: I found a watch.
我找到一隻錶。

B: Whose is it?
這是誰的？

💬 **也可以這樣用：**

A: This is a nice book.
這是一本很好的書。

B: Whose is it?
是誰寫的？

16. **When are you paying me back?** 你什麼時候還我錢？

💬 確切地表明歸還時間：

A: When are you paying me back?
你什麼時候還我錢？

B: Next month.
下個月。

💬 真的沒有錢：

A: When are you paying me back?
你什麼時候還我錢？

B: I am sorry. I'm still tight with money.
對不起，我的手頭還是很緊。

17. **No way!** 不行！

💬 斷然回絕請求：

A: Can you lend me your car?
你可不可以借我你的車？

B: No way! Remember what you did to it last time?
不行！你記得上一次你做了什麼好事嗎？

💬 表明喜好：

A: Let's have pizza for lunch.
我們中午去吃披薩。

B: No way! I hate pizza.
才不要呢！我討厭披薩。

💬 更直接的說法：

No way! I won't help you.
不行！我不會幫你。

18. **Not in your lifetime!** 門都沒有！

💬 痴人說夢：

A: May I borrow your car?
我可以跟你借車嗎？

B: Not in your lifetime! You don't even have a license.
門都沒有！你連駕照都沒有！

💬 不給任何機會：

A: Could I ask you out?
我可以邀你出去嗎？

B: Not in your lifetime!
門都沒有！

* li·cense	['laɪsns]	名	執照

19. **Never mind.** 沒關係；不要緊。

💬 原諒別人的無心之過：

A: I am sorry that I broke your radio.
對不起，我把你的收音機弄壞了。

B: Never mind.
沒關係。

💬 不介意，表示原諒：

A: I forgot to bring your book.
我忘記把你的書帶來了。

B: Never mind.
沒關係。

💬 不用在意，小事一件：

Never mind. It's not a big *deal*.
沒關係，這沒什麼。

* deal	[dil]	名	買賣、交易

Chapter 02 人際社交 Interpersonal Relationships

🐱 Chat 不斷流

Layla 萊拉	Pretty shoes. Whose are they? 這雙鞋真美，是誰的？
Brian 布萊恩	My girlfriend's. I bought her these. 我買給我女朋友的。
Layla 萊拉	That's sweet. How much are they? 你真好，這雙鞋多少錢？
Brian 布萊恩	They cost me six hundred bucks. 花了我六百美金。
Layla 萊拉	No way! 不會吧！
Brian 布萊恩	Do you think you could lend me some money? I am a little tight with money. 你能借我一些錢嗎？我手頭有點緊。
Layla 萊拉	How much do you want? 你想借多少？
Brian 布萊恩	Maybe eight hundred? 也許八百元？
Layla 萊拉	Absolutely out of the question! 想都別想！
Brian 布萊恩	Six hundred dollars then? 那六百元呢？
Layla 萊拉	When are you paying me back? 你準備什麼時候還我錢？
Brian 布萊恩	At the end of this year? 年底？
Layla 萊拉	Not in your lifetime! 門都沒有！
Brian 布萊恩	Alright, never mind. I'll turn to somebody else for help. 好吧，算了，我去找別人幫忙。

20. **Bon voyage.** 一路順風。

💬 **有朋遠行，由衷祝福：**

A: We are leaving for Boston tonight.
我們今晚要出發去波士頓。

B: Bon voyage.
一路順風。

💬 **期待再相見：**

A: Bye! Bon voyage!
再見！一路順風。

B: See you next year.
明年見囉！

💬 **朋友出遊，你可以這樣說：**

Bon voyage and have fun!
一路順風、好好玩！

21. **Have fun.** 玩得盡興點。

💬 **快樂旅程出發：**

A: We're leaving for the *beach*.
我們要向海邊出發了。

B: Have fun.
玩得盡興點。

💬 **送上祝福：**

A: Have fun on your *honeymoon*.
祝你們蜜月旅行玩得愉快。

B: Thank you.
謝謝。

* beach	[bitʃ]	名	海灘
* hon·ey·moon	[ˈhʌnɪˌmun]	名	蜜月

Chapter 02 人際社交 *Interpersonal Relationships*

22. **It's a pity.** 真可惜。

💬 **實在很可惜：**

A: Jimmy is sick. He won't be able to come.
吉米生病了，他不能來了。

B: It's a pity.
真可惜。

💬 **真心覺得遺憾：**

A: It's a pity that Jill and Leslie are *filing* for a divorce.
吉兒和賴斯力要申請離婚真可惜。

B: Yes, they were so much in love.
對啊，他們以前很恩愛。

💬 **感嘆離別：**

It's a pity that you are going to leave.
真可惜你要走了。

* file	[faɪl]	動	提出（申請）；歸檔

23. **Step aside.** 讓開。

💬 **借過：**

A: Please step aside. You are *blocking* my way.
請讓開，你擋住我了！

B: Sorry! 對不起。

💬 **不客氣的說法：**

A: Step aside! I'm coming through!
讓開！我要過來了。

B: You are such a bully! 你真霸道！

💬 **沒有禮貌：**

Step aside! You are in my way.
讓開！你擋到我了。

* block	[blɑk]	動	阻塞

24. **That's all right.**　沒關係。

💬 對方忘記了所託之事：

A: Sorry, I forgot to buy salt.
對不起，我忘記買鹽了。

B: That's all right.
沒關係。

💬 不是故意的：

A: I didn't mean to ***bump*** into you.
我不是故意撞到你的。

B: That's all right.
沒關係。

💬 讓對方安心：

That's alright. I'll solve the problem.
沒關係，我會解決這個問題。

* bump	[bʌmp]	動	碰、撞

25. **Please don't be mad at me.**　請不要生我的氣。

💬 坦誠從寬：

A: I am going to tell you the ***truth***, but please don't be mad at me.
我要跟你說實話，但請別生我的氣。

B: Only if you tell the ***truth***.
除非你說實話。

💬 請求諒解：

A: Please don't be mad at me. I really didn't mean it.
請不要生我的氣，我真的不是故意的。

B: Fine. Don't do it again.
好吧！別再這麼做了。

* truth	[truθ]	名	真相、真理

26. **Not again!** 不會吧！

💬 **難以相信、無法接受：**

A: We've been *cheated*.
我們被騙了。

B: Not again!
不會吧！

💬 **難以置信：**

A: Everyone's late.
每個人都遲到了。

B: Not again!
不會吧！

* cheat	[tʃit]	動	欺騙

27. **(It) beats me.** 我想不出來；我不知道。

💬 **遇到難題時：**

A: Do you know the *height* of that *building*?
你知道那大樓的高度嗎？

B: It beats me.
你考倒我了。

💬 **：沒有人知道**

A: I wonder where they went.
我不知道他們去哪裡了。

B: Beats me.
我也不知道。

💬 **還可以這樣說：**

It beats me. You can ask others.
這考倒我了，你可以問問看別人。

* height	[haɪt]	名	高度
* build·ing	[ˈbɪldɪn]	名	建築物

28. **You got me!** 你考倒我了！

💬 幫不上忙：

A: Do you know how to solve this problem?
你知道如何解決這個問題嗎？

B: You got me! I really don't know.
你考倒我了，我真的不知道。

💬 沒有頭緒的時候：

A: Which way should we go?
我該往哪裡走呢？

B: You got me! I have no idea.
你考倒我了，我不知道。

💬 也可以這樣回答：

You got me! The question is so hard.
你考倒我了！這問題真是難。

* solve	[sɑlv]	動	解決

29. **That's enough.** 夠了！

💬 太多了，超出負荷：

A: That's enough. I can't finish up this chicken noodle soup.
夠了，我沒辦法把這碗雞湯麵全部吃完。

B: Yes, you can.
你可以吃完的。

💬 忍無可忍：

A: That's enough. I've had enough of you.
夠了，我受夠你了。

B: Please let me explain.
請讓我解釋。

💬 受不了對方：

That's enough of you.
你真的夠了。

Chapter 02 人際社交 Interpersonal Relationships

🐱Chat 不斷流

Liz 莉茲	Have you seen my blue dress? 你有看到我的藍洋裝嗎？
Alison 愛莉森	No, I haven't. Sorry! 沒有耶，抱歉。
Liz 莉茲	I can't find it, and I'm leaving for the airport in an hour! 我找不到它，而且我一個小時內就要出發到機場了！
Alison 愛莉森	It's a pity that you can't bring it with you to the States. It's such a beautiful dress. 你不能帶它去美國真可惜，那件洋裝很美。
Liz 莉茲	Oh, never mind. I might not even have the occasion to wear it anyway. 算了，沒關係，也許我根本不會有適合的場合穿它。
Alison 愛莉森	Do you mind me wearing it if I happen to find it some day? 如果有一天我找到這件洋裝，你介意我拿來穿嗎？
Liz 莉茲	Not in your life time! 門都沒有！
Alison 愛莉森	Why? You won't be able to wear it in a year! 為什麼？反正你這一年都穿不到！
Liz 莉茲	I was just kidding! I don't mind. I think it'll look gorgeous on you, too. 跟你開玩笑的，我不介意，我覺得你穿也會很美。
Alison 愛莉森	Thanks, Liz. You're very kind! 謝謝，莉茲，你真大方。
Liz 莉茲	No problem. I've got to go. See you next summer! 沒問題，我要走了，明年夏天見！
Alison 愛莉森	Hope you have a wonderful school year. Bon voyage! 祝你新學年過得順心，一路順風！

30. **You asked for it.** 你自找的。

💬 **勿以小惡而為之：**

A: It's so ***humiliating*** when the bus driver found I was trying to jump the bus.
當司機發現我企圖逃票時，真是糗。

B: You asked for it!
這可是你自找的喔！

💬 **大嘴巴被發現：**

A: She ***yelled*** at me when she found I was telling about her ***secret***.
當她發現我在說她的祕密時，她對我大聲怒罵。

B: You asked for it!
是你自找的。

* hu·mil·i·ate	[hjuˋmɪlɪˌet]	動	侮辱、羞辱
* yell	[jɛl]	動	大叫、呼喊
* se·cret	[ˋsikrɪt]	名	祕密

31. **So what?** 那又如何？那又怎樣？

💬 **不以為然：**

A: Do you know there is a new ***theater*** down the street?
你知道街上開了一家新的戲院嗎？

B: Yeah. So what?
知道啊，那又怎麼樣呢？

💬 **然後呢：**

A: Remember the books you lent me last week?
你記得你上禮拜借我的書嗎？

B: Of course. So what?
當然囉，那又怎麼樣呢？

So what? What do you exactly mean?
所以呢？你到底是什麼意思？

* the·a·ter	[ˈθiətə]	名	戲院、劇場

🎧 *Track 191*

32. Nonsense!　胡說八道！

對於誇張的事物予以駁斥：

A: I can hold my breath for half an hour.
　　我可以憋住呼吸半小時。

B: Nonsense! You will die by then.
　　胡說八道！你那樣會死掉。

要求聽實話：

A: Tell me the truth. I don't want any nonsense.
　　告訴我實話，我不要聽胡說八道的話。

B: I am telling the truth.
　　我是說實話啊。

想聽真話：

I don't like to hear nonsense.
我不想聽胡說八道。

🎧 *Track 192*

33. Better left unsaid.　還是別說好了。

探聽別人的隱私：

A: So what happened to your friend who *stole* money from his company?
　　你那個偷公司錢的朋友現在怎麼樣？

B: Better left unsaid.
　　還是別說的好。

💬 說八卦：

A: Did Mary really have an *affair* with her boss?
　　瑪麗和他的老闆真的有婚外情嗎？

B: It's better left unsaid.
　　還是別說的好。

* steal	[stil]	動	偷、騙取
* af·fair	[əˋfɛr]	名	事件

34. I am speechless.　我無話可說。

💬 **感動地無以言喻：**

A: Hi, I got you some flowers.
　　嗨！我帶了一些花給你。

B: I am speechless.
　　我不知道該說什麼！

💬 **百口莫辯：**

A: I caught you with another woman.
　　我抓到你和別的女人在一起。

B: I am speechless.
　　我無話可說。

🎧 *Track 194*

35. I am speechless.　我無話可說。

💬 **心有餘而力不足：**

A: I felt so bad. I can't do anything to help her.
　　我覺得好難過，我沒法為她做任何事。

B: You've done all you can.
　　你已經竭盡所能了。

💬 **無可奈何：**

A: Sandy never *reflects* on herself.
　　珊迪從來不反省她自己。

B: Well, I can't do anything.
　　嗯，我也沒辦法。

Chapter 02 人際社交 Interpersonal Relationships

💬 難過地自責：

I can't do anything to stop this war.
我無能為力停止這戰爭。

* re·flect	[rɪˈflɛkt]	動	反省

🎧 *Track 195*

36. *Hang* in there.　堅持下去。

💬 加油打氣很重要：

Don't give up now! *Hang* in there.
現在別放棄啊！堅持下去！

💬 支持鼓勵不能少：

Hang in there. I know you will make it.
堅持下去，我知道你會成功的。

* hang	[hæŋ]	動	吊、掛

🎧 *Track 196*

37. take care　保重

💬 離情依依：

A: Remember to take care of yourself when you get there.
　　你去到那邊要保重自己。

B: I know. You, too.
　　我會的。你也是！

💬 互道珍重：

A: Bye! Take care.
　　再見！保重。

B: See you.
　　再見！

💬 千叮萬囑：

Take care of yourself after leaving.
你離開這裡之後要好好保重。

38. **I know what you mean.** 我知道你的意思。

💬 **無法接受事實：**

A: How could Becky do something like that?
　　貝琪怎麼可以做出那種事啊？

B: I know what you mean. But it's really not her *fault*.
　　我知道你的意思，可是那真的不是她的錯。

💬 **同理心：**

A: Do you understand me?
　　你知道我的意思嗎？

B: I know what you mean.
　　我知道你的意思。

💬 **理解但無法認同：**

I know what you mean but I *disagree*.
我懂你的意思但我不贊同。

* fault	[fɔlt]	名	責任、過失
* dis·a·gree	[dɪsəˈgri]	動	不認同

39. **Got it.** 收到；了解。

💬 **表示理解：**

A: You have to get this done by tomorrow.
　　你明天以前一定得把這做好。

B: Got it.
　　收到。

💬 **拿到東西了：**

A: Did you take your keys?
　　你有沒有拿你的鑰匙？

B: Got it.
　　拿了。

🐱 Chat 不斷流

Hilary 希拉蕊	I am speechless. 我不知道該説什麼！
Hailey 海莉	What's the matter? 怎麼了？
Hilary 希拉蕊	It's better left unsaid. 還是別説的好。
Hailey 海莉	Is it about your boyfriend, Joel, again? 又為了妳男朋友喬而煩惱？
Hilary 希拉蕊	Nonsense! 胡説！
Hailey 海莉	What then? 那是怎麼回事？
Hilary 希拉蕊	A girl in school stole my best friend. 有個女生搶走我最好的朋友。
Hailey 海莉	So what? Go make some new friends! 又怎樣？去交新朋友就好啦！
Hilary 希拉蕊	But she and I have been friend for five years. 但我們這五年來都是最好的朋友。
Hailey 海莉	I know what you mean. 我懂你的感受。
Hilary 希拉蕊	And she doesn't care at all! 她完全不在乎。
Hailey 海莉	That's a shame. Sorry, I can't do anything to help. 很遺憾，抱歉，我沒辦法幫你。
Hilary 希拉蕊	That's alright. 沒關係。
Hailey 海莉	Hang in there! 撐下去吧。
Hilary 希拉蕊	Thanks, I will. 我會的，謝謝。

40. **Do you mind...** 你介意……？

💬 **詢問旁人的意願：**

A: Do you mind if I sit beside you?
你介意我坐你旁邊嗎？

B: Of course not. Take a seat.
當然不會囉。請坐。

💬 **禮貌性地要求對方：**

A: Do you mind not *chewing* so loud?
你介意不要吃的那麼大聲嗎？

B: Oh, I am sorry about that.
對不起。

💬 **請求知道對方的想法：**

Do you mind telling me when you are free?
介意告訴我你何時有空嗎？

| * chew | [tʃu] | 動 | 咀嚼 |

41. **Do you know...?** 你知道……嗎？

💬 **表示關心：**

A: Do you know what happened to him?
你知道他怎麼了嗎？

B: No. What's wrong?
不知道耶，怎麼了？

💬 **有疑問時：**

A: Do you know the way to the town *center*?
你知道怎麼去鎮中心嗎？

B: I am sorry I don't.
對不起，我不知道。

💬 **也可以這樣問：**

Do you know when we'll go back?
你知道我們什麼時候會回去嗎？

* cen·ter	[ˈsɛntə]	名	中心、中央

🎧 *Track 202*

42. I feel that...　我覺得……

💬 心裡有疑問：

A: I feel that you don't care about me anymore.
我覺得你不再關心我了。

B: But I do.
可是我在乎。

💭 身體感官變化：

A: I feel that today is colder than *yesterday*.
我覺得今天比昨天冷。

B: Then you should wear a coat.
所以你應該穿件外套。

💬 表達想法：

I feel that you really like her.
我覺得你真的很喜歡她。

* yes·ter·day	[ˈjɛstəde]	名	昨天、昨日

🎧 *Track 203*

43. And you?　你呢？

💬 想要吃什麼：

A: I want a cheeseburger. And you?
我要一個起司漢堡，你呢？

B: I will have a hotdog.
我要一個熱狗。

💭 詢問意見：

A: I am not hungry. I will just have a cup of coffee. And you?
我不是很餓，我只要一杯咖啡，你呢？

B: Me, too.
我也是。

44. *count* **me out**　不要算我（我不參加）

💬 **超出預算：**

A: The trip will cost each of us $10,000.
這趟旅行每一個人將要出 $10,000

B: I don't have that much money. *Count* me out!
我沒那麼多錢，我不參加了！

💬 **迫於無奈：**

Count me out of the game tomorrow. My legs are killing me.
明天的比賽我不參加，我的腿痛死了。

* count	[kaʊnt]	動	計數

45. **I am outspoken.**　我講話直了些。

💬 **不小心冒犯了：**

A: Why was Ms. Lee so *mad* in class this morning?
李老師今天早上上課時為什麼那麼生氣啊？

B: I was outspoken, and it made him so angry.
因為我講話直了些，而使得他勃然大怒。

💬 **說話不經思考：**

A: You shouldn't have said that.
你不應該那樣說的。

B: Sorry, I was outspoken.
對不起，我說話直了些。

💬 **表達太直白：**

I am outspoken but I didn't mean to say that.
我講話直了點，但我不是故意這樣說的。

* mad	[mæd]	形	神經錯亂的、發瘋的

Chapter 02 人際社交 Interpersonal Relationships

46. **It suddenly** *strikes* **me...**　我突然想到……

💬 **忽然就冒出了好點子：**

A: Wait! It suddenly *strikes* me that we can go to Kenting this weekend.
等等！我突然想到我們這週末可以去墾丁。

B: Yeah. Good idea.
對啊！好主意。

💬 **靈光乍現：**

A: How did you come up with your new idea?
你是怎麼想到你的新點子的？

B: It just suddenly *struck* me.
我突然想到的。

💬 **差一點忘記：**

It suddenly strikes me that today is your birthday.
我突然想到今天是你的生日。

* strike	[straɪk]	動	打擊、達成（協議）

47. **What's on** *tap* **for today?**　今天有什麼事要完成的？

💬 **無所事事的時候：**

A: What's on *tap* for today?
今天有什麼事要完成的？

B: Nothing much.
沒什麼。

💬 **確認進度：**

A: What's on *tap* for today?
今天有什麼事要完成的？

B: We have to finish the project today.
我們今天要做完這個計畫案。

* tap	[tæp]	名	水龍頭

48. It's acceptable. 可以接受的。

💬 **探試別人的觀感：**

A: How was my report?
我的報告如何？

B: It's acceptable.
還可以接受。

💬 **達成協議：**

A: I will give you this ring if you help me.
你如果幫我，我就把這個戒指給你。

B: Sounds *fair*. It's acceptable.
公平啊，可以接受。

💬 **取代得到認同：**

It's acceptable that you take her position.
你代替她的位子是可接受的。

| * fair | [fɛr] | 形 | 公平的、合理的 |

49. Over my dead body! 想都別想（除非我死了）！

💬 **沒有一點點的可能性：**

A: Can I borrow your car?
我可不可以跟你借車？

B: Over my dead body! You just *totaled* my last one!
想都別想，你把我上部車撞爛了。

💬 **表達堅決的反對立場：**

A: Dad, can I please marry George?
爸，我可不可以嫁給喬治？

B: Over my dead body! I am not going to let my daughter marry
someone who can't even feed himself.
想想別想！我不會把我女兒嫁給一個連自己都餵不飽的人。

| * to·tal | ['totl] | 動 | 將（汽車）徹底撞毀 |

Chapter 02 人際社交 Interpersonal Relationships

113

🐱 Chat 不斷流

Jessica 潔西卡	What's on tap for today? 今天有什麼事要完成的？
Brett 布瑞特	Nothing, really. 沒什麼。
Jessica 潔西卡	Cool, how about we go out for dinner tonight? 酷，我們今晚去吃飯如何？
Brett 布瑞特	Actually... Do you mind if I go out with the guys tonight? 老實說……你介意我今晚跟朋友出去嗎？
Jessica 潔西卡	Where are the guys going? 你們要去哪？
Brett 布瑞特	We are going to a football game. 我們要去看足球賽。
Jessica 潔西卡	Oh, alright. Count me out! 好吧，我不參加。
Brett 布瑞特	Why don't you come? 你為什麼不一起來？
Jessica 潔西卡	I don't like football. Also, your friend, Cole creeps me out. 我不喜歡足球，而且你朋友柯爾讓我渾身不自在。
Brett 布瑞特	I feel that you don't like any of my friends. 你好像不喜歡我任何一位朋友。
Jessica 潔西卡	That's not the case. 才不是這樣。
Brett 布瑞特	But I was thinking of inviting him to our wedding. 但我還想說要邀請他來參加我們的婚禮。
Jessica 潔西卡	Over my dead body! 想都別想！

50. Let me tell you...　讓我告訴你……

💬 指點迷津：

A: I don't know how to get to the station.
我不知道怎麼去車站？

B: Let me tell you the way.
讓我告訴你路線吧！

💬 當別人心中納悶時：

A: Why did she give me the cold shoulder?
她為什麼對我那麼冷淡？

B: Let me tell you the reason.
讓我告訴你原因吧！

💬 揭曉答案：

Let me tell you why she is not here.
讓我告訴你為什麼她不在這裡。

51. go fifty-fifty on something　平分

💬 一起出遊共同分擔費用：

A: How should we pay for the travel *fee*?
我們旅遊的錢要怎麼出？

B: Let's go fifty-fifty on it.
我們平分吧！

💬 平攤比較好算：

Let's go fifty-fifty on dinner.
我們晚餐費用平均分攤。

* fee	[fi]	名	費用

Chapter 02 人際社交 Interpersonal Relationships

52. **Cut it out!**　別鬧了！（停止打鬥、爭吵等）

💬 保持安靜：

A: Cut it out! The baby is sleeping.
別鬧了！小嬰兒在睡覺。

B: Sorry about that.
對不起。

💬 專注工作，確保進度完成：

A: Cut it out! We have to get this done by Tuesday.
別再鬧了！我們星期二前要做完耶！

B: Don't worry. We still have *plenty* of time.
別擔心，我們多的是時間。

💬 不要再胡鬧了：

Cut it out! The room is already a mess.
別再鬧了！房間已經一團亂了。

* plen·ty	[ˋplɛntɪ]	形	充足的

53. **Knock it off!**　住手！不要吵！

💬 請讓我專心念書：

A: Knock it off! I am trying to study.
別吵了！我要讀書耶！

B: Sorry, I didn't know that you are studying.
對不起，我不知道你在讀書。

💬 不要這樣做：

A: Knock it off!
住手！

B: I was just trying to pull this grey hair out.
我只是想幫你把這根白頭髮拔出來。

Knock it off! Don't touch it.
住手！別碰！

54. Talk to you later.　待會兒再跟你談。

先忙別的事，等一下再說：

A: I need to go now. Talk to you later.
　　我現在得走了，等會兒再跟你談。

B: Bye.
　　再見。

會議就要開始了：

A: The meeting will be held in three more minutes.
　　會議將在三分鐘左右後開始。

B: OK. I will talk to you later then.
　　好，我待會兒再跟你談吧！

也可以這樣說：

I have a meeting in a minute. Talk to you later.
我現在馬上有個會議，等會兒再跟你談。

55. take my word for it　相信我的話

我保證：

A: You said that restaurant *serves* really good food?
　　你說那家餐廳的餐點真的很好吃？

B: Yeah, you could take my word for it.
　　是啊！你可以相信我的話！

真心推薦：

She's a great doctor. You should take my word for it.
你相信我，她是一個很棒的醫生。

* serve	[sɝv]	動	服務、招待

56. **Get real!** 別鬧了；別開玩笑了！

💬 **怎麼可能？說笑的吧：**

A: Do you want to join the swim team with me?
你要不要和我一起加入游泳隊？

B: Me, swim team? Get real!
我加入游泳隊？別開玩笑了？

💬 **要準備開會了：**

A: Maybe your boss will give you a *raise* this month.
也許你老闆這個月會為你加薪喔。

B: Get real! My boss is a miser.
別開玩笑了，我老闆是一個小氣鬼。

* raise	[rez]	名	加薪

57. **Let it be.** 就這樣吧！

💬 **這樣就很好了：**

A: Should I take out the logo sticker on this page?
我要不要把這頁的商標拿掉？

B: No, let it be. It looks pretty good.
不，就這樣吧！它看起來不錯。

💬 **不要管他：**

A: What should we do to stop the baby from crying?
我們該怎麼讓小嬰兒停止哭泣呢？

B: Let it be.
讓他去吧。

💬 **隨便他：**

Let it be. I don't mind.
讓他去吧，我不在意。

58. *Suit* yourself.　隨你高興。

💬 **與我無關：**

A: I want to eat three hamburgers for lunch.
我中餐想吃三個漢堡。

B: *Suit* yourself.
隨便你！

💬 **沒關係，你好就好：**

A: I am too tired to go to the movies with you tonight.
今天晚上我太累了，不能跟你去看電影。

B: *Suit* yourself! I will ask John to go with me.
隨你高興囉！那我叫約翰陪我去！

* suit	[sut]	動	適合

59. What's the catch?　有什麼意圖？

💬 **怎麼突然那麼好：**

A: Do you need me to help you with anything?
你需不需要我幫你做什麼事啊？

B: What's the catch?
你有什麼意圖？

💬 **禮多必詐：**

Why is Harry so nice to me all of a *sudden*? What's the catch?
哈利為什麼突然對我那麼好？有什麼意圖？

* sud·den	[ˈsʌdn]	名	意外、突然

Chapter 02 人際社交 *Interpersonal Relationships*

🐱 Chat 不 斷 流

Jerry 傑瑞	How about we go out for a drink tonight? 我們今晚一起去喝東西如何？
Jenny 珍妮	Are we going fifty-fifty on the drinks? 酒錢平分嗎？
Jerry 傑瑞	Nah. All on me. 不用，我會請你。
Jenny 珍妮	Really? How come? What's the catch? 真的嗎？為什麼？你有什麼意圖？
Jerry 傑瑞	I have a secret to tell. 我想跟你說一個祕密。
Jenny 珍妮	Just tell me here! 在這跟我說就好了。
Jerry 傑瑞	Alright, suit yourself. 好吧，隨你高興。
Jenny 珍妮	What is it? 祕密是什麼？
Jerry 傑瑞	Angela has won a million dollars. 安琪拉中了一百萬。
Jenny 珍妮	Get real! 別開玩笑了！
Jerry 傑瑞	Just take my word for it. She told me about it herself. 相信我，這是她自己跟我說的。
Jenny 珍妮	Well, good for her! 那她還真幸運。

60. So happy to see you. 真高興見到你。

💬 **認識新朋友：**

A: Hi!
嗨！

B: So happy to see you.
真高興見到你。

💬 **再次重逢的喜悅：**

A: Long time no see.
好久不見。

B: So happy to see you.
真高興見到你。

💬 **相見歡：**

I'm happy to see you here.
很開心在這裡見到你。

61. I'm just thinking about it. 只是想想罷了。

💬 **想改變主意：**

A: Are you going to change your mind?
你要改變主意了嗎？

B: I'm just thinking about it.
只是想想罷了。

💬 **躍躍欲試：**

A: Do you really want to do that?
你真的想做那件事嗎？

B: I'm just thinking about it.
只是想想罷了。

💬 **尚未付諸行動：**

I'm just thinking about it, but I haven't made a *decision* yet.
只是想想罷了，但是我還沒決定。

* de·ci·sion	[dɪˈsɪʒən]	名	決定、決斷力

62. **There you go!　請便！**

💬 **同意他人使用：**

A: May I play with this?
我可以玩這個嗎？

B: There you go!
請便！

💬 **沒問題，請自便：**

A: Can I see this?
我可以看這個嗎？

B: There you go!
請便！

63. **Is there anything I can help you with?**
有什麼我可以幫忙的嗎？

💬 **主動釋放善意：**

A: Is there anything I can help you with?
有什麼我可以幫忙的嗎？

B: No, I'm fine.
沒有關係，我可以。

💬 **伸出援手：**

A: Is there anything I can help you with?
有什麼我可以幫忙的嗎？

B: Yes, please.
有的，麻煩你。

64. **I'll be right there.　馬上來。**

💬 **立刻過去：**

A: Come quickly!
快點來！

B: I'll be right there.
馬上來。

💬 **快到了哦：**

A: Are you coming?
　你要來了嗎？

B: Yes, I'll be right there.
　是的，馬上來。

💬 **再等一下下：**

Please wait for a minute. I'll be there soon.
請等我一分鐘，我馬上來。

🎧 *Track 227*

65. Hurry up!　快一點！

💬 **要遲到了：**

A: Hurry up! You are going to be late for school.
　快一點，你上學要遲到了。

B: Coming, coming.
　來了，來了。

💬 **催促動作加快：**

A: Hurry up, James. We are all *waiting* for you.
　詹姆斯快一點，我們大家都在等你。

B: Sorry.
　對不起。

💬 **快要來不及了：**

Hurry up. We are late.
快一點，我們遲到了。

* wait	[wet]	動	等待

66. let the cat out of the bag 洩漏祕密

💬 **指出透漏消息者：**

A: How did Lisa know about this?
　　莎莉怎麼知道這件事的？

B: Bill let the cat out of the bag.
　　是比爾洩漏祕密的。

💬 **是誰說出來的：**

A: Who let the cat out of the bag?
　　是誰洩密的？

B: It was Tim.
　　是提姆。

67. You can say so. 可以這麼說啦！

💬 **回答模稜兩可：**

A: Is he a *special* friend?
　　他是一個特別的朋友嗎？

B: You can say so.
　　可以這麼說啦！

💬 **算是吧：**

A: He's the fastest runner in school.
　　他是全校跑最快的。

B: You can say so.
　　可以這麼說啦！

| * spe·cial | [ˈspɛʃəl] | 形 | 專門的、特別的 |

68. I think we have met somewhere. 我想我們在哪裡見過。

💬 **覺得很面熟：**

A: I think we have met somewhere.
　　我想我們在哪裡見過。

B: You look really *familiar*.
你看起來很熟悉。

💬 **想不起來對方是誰時：**

A: I think we have met somewhere.
我想我們在哪裡見過。

B: I am your Aunt Betty, don't you remember?
我是你的貝蒂阿姨，你不記得了嗎？

| * fa·mil·iar | [fəˋmɪljɚ] | 形 | 熟悉的、親密的 |

🎧 *Track 231*

69. **That really burns me up!** 那真的惹毛我了！

💬 **超級不爽：**

A: Why are you so mad?
你為什麼那麼生氣？

B: He *poured* water on me. That really burns me up!
他向我潑水。那真的惹火我了！

💬 **怒火中燒：**

A: That really burns me up! I am going to *confront* her.
那真的惹火我了！我要去跟她對質。

B: You should calm down first.
你應該先冷靜。

| * pour | [por] | 動 | 澆、倒 |
| * con·front | [kənˋfrʌnt] | 動 | 面對、面臨 |

Chapter 02 人際社交 Interpersonal Relationships

🐾 Chat 不斷流

Jonah 強納	Hey there, ma'am, is there anything I can help you with? 你好，女士，有什麼我可以幫忙的嗎？
Angie 安琪	Yes, could you please get the box on the top shelf for me? I can't seem to reach it. 是的，能請你幫我拿上層的盒子嗎？我拿不到。
Jonah 強納	Sure, I'll be right there. 當然好，我馬上過去。
Angie 安琪	Thanks, but hurry up, please. I've got to go pick up my kids from school. 謝謝，但麻煩快一點，我還要去學校接小孩。
Jonah 強納	Okay... there you go. Here's the box you wanted. 好的，拿去吧，這是你要的箱子。
Angie 安琪	Thanks! 謝謝！
Jonah 強納	Hey, wait a minute... I think we have met somewhere. 等等……我想我們在哪裡見過。
Angie 安琪	Really? I don't think so. 真的嗎？我不這麼認為。
Jonah 強納	Didn't we go to university together? Angie, right? 我們不是一起上大學嗎？你是安琪，對吧？
Angie 安琪	Yeah, are you Jordan? 是啊，你是喬丹吧？
Jonah 強納	It's Jonah. I'm so happy to see you. 是強納，真高興見到你。
Angie 安琪	Oh right, Jonah. Same here. I didn't expect to see you again! 噢對，你是強納，我也是，沒想到我們會再見面！

126

70. beat a dead horse　白費勁

💬 **一切都太晚了：**

A: I think we need to talk about it more.
　　我覺得我們需要再談談這件事。

B: You are beating a dead horse. It's already *settled*.
　　你是在白費勁吧！這件事已經定了。

💬 **緣木求魚，徒勞無功：**

You are beating a dead horse *borrowing* money from him. He is a miser
你跟他借錢簡直是白費勁！他是一個小氣鬼。

* set·tle	[ˈsɛtl̩]	動	安排、解決
* bor·row	[ˈbɑro]	動	借來、採用

71. once in a blue moon　千載難逢；難得一次

💬 **百年難得一見：**

A: Did you see the old lady living next door?
　　你有沒有看到住你家隔壁的老太太？

B: Only once in a blue moon.
　　難得一次。

💬 **久久一次：**

A: I go to the *gym* once in a blue moon.
　　我很久才去一次健身房。

B: You should work out more.
　　你應該多運動！

* gym	[dʒɪm]	名	體育館、健身房

Chapter 02 人際社交 Interpersonal Relationships

72. Better luck next time.　下次運氣更好。

💬 **風水輪流轉：**

A: I lost $2000 playing mah-jong last night.
我昨晚打麻將輸了 2000 元。

B: Better luck next time.
下一次運氣會比較好。

💬 **下一次勝利一定屬於我們：**

A: I can't believe that we lost the game.
我不敢相信我們輸了這場球賽！

B: Better luck next time. Don't worry.
下一次運氣會更好。別擔心！

73. (There's) no way to tell.　沒辦法知道。

💬 **毫無頭緒：**

A: Do you think the Red Socks will win the game tonight?
你覺得紅襪隊今晚會贏嗎？

B: There's no way to tell now.
現在沒辦法知道。

💬 **變數太大，無法預估：**

A: How long will it take us to get to grandma's house?
去外婆家還需要多久啊？

B: There's no way to tell from this *traffic* jam.
沒辦法知道，現在交通很糟糕。

* traf·fic	['træfɪk]	名	交通

74. read someone like an *open* book　清楚某人心裡的想法

💬 **洞察他人心性：**

A: How do you know John will come?
你怎麼知道約翰會來？

B: That's because I read him like an *open* book.
因為我太了解他了。

💬 表示同理心：

After all these years, I can read you like an *open* book. I know you aren't happy.
經過這些年我對你很了解，我知道你不開心。

* o·pen	[ˈopən]	形	開的、公開的

🎧 *Track 238*

75. on the tip of one's *tongue*
差一點就說出口；差一點就記起來的

💬 快要想起來了：

I don't remember her name. It was on the tip of my *tongue*.
我不記得她的名字了，我差一點點就要記起來了。

💬 差點說溜嘴：

A: That plan is a secret.
那個計畫是一個祕密。

B: Luckily, I didn't say anything. It was on the tip of my *tongue*.
還好，我什麼都沒說，我差一點就要說出口了。

* tongue	[tʌŋ]	名	舌、舌頭

🎧 *Track 239*

76. Do you have any change?　你有零錢嗎？

💬 可以跟你換零錢嗎：

A: Do you have any change? I am going to take a bus.
你有零錢嗎？我需要搭公車。

B: Sorry, I don't.　對不起，我沒有。

💬 朋友有通財之義：

A: Do you have any change? I want to get a coke.
你有零錢嗎？我要買可樂。

B: Get me one, too.　幫我也買一個吧。

77. **Could you *lend* me some money?** 可以借我點錢嗎？

💬 同是天涯淪落人：

A: Could you *lend* me some money?
你可以借我一點錢嗎？

B: Sorry. I am broke myself.
對不起，我自己也破產了。

💬 慷慨解囊：

A: Could you *lend* me some money?
你可以借我一點錢嗎？

B: Sure! How much do you need?
沒問題！你需要多少錢？

* lend	[lɛnd]	動	借出

78. **Who do you think you are?** 你以為你是誰啊？

💬 遇到無理要求時：

A: Move! I want to sit here.
走開，我要坐在這裡。

B: Who do you think you are?
你以為你是誰啊？

💬 不要對我頤指氣使：

A: Hey, go get my *slippers* for me.
喂！去幫我拿拖鞋來！

B: Who do you think you are?
你以為你是誰啊？

* slip·per(s)	[ˈslɪpɚ(z)]	名	拖鞋

79. Send my *regards* to...or me.　代我問候。

💬 **順便問候他人：**

A: See you next time.
下次見！

B: Bye! Send my *regards* to Kelly for me.
再見，替我向凱利問好。

💬 **未能見面深表遺憾：**

A: It was a pity that Helen didn't come. Remember to send my *regards* to her for me.
海倫沒來真可惜，記得幫我跟她問好。

B: Sure, I will.
當然，我會的。

💬 **務必轉達心意：**

Send my *regards* to Susan for me next time.
下次請代我跟蘇珊問好。

* re·gard	[rɪˋgɑrd]	名	注視

📱Chat 不 斷 流

Amber 安柏	Could you lend me some money? 可以借我點錢嗎？
Sharon 雪倫	How much do you want? 你想借多少錢？
Amber 安柏	Just some change. Do you have any change? 一些零錢就好，你有零錢嗎？
Sharon 雪倫	Yeah. I've got about 40 dollars. 我有大約四十元。

Amber 安柏	That'll do. 夠了。
Sharon 雪倫	Are you thinking of getting some candy on the way home? 你是不是想在回家的路上買糖果？
Amber 安柏	Exactly. How do you know? 沒錯，你怎麼知道？
Sharon 雪倫	I can read you like an open book. 我很清楚你心裡的想法
Amber 安柏	No way! I buy candy only once in a blue moon. 才怪，我難得買糖果。

🎧 *Track 244*

80. I've been through it.　我領教過了。

💬 **已經有經驗了：**

A: She is so unreasonable.
　她很不講理。

B: I've been through it.
　我領教過了。

💭 **也可以這樣用：**

A: She has a bad *temper*.
　她脾氣很壞。

B: I've been through it.
　我領教過了。

* tem·per	['tɛmpɚ]	名	脾氣

81. The more, the *merrier*.　越多越好。

💬 歡迎更多人參加：

A: Can I bring my friends to the party?
我可以帶朋友來參加這個派對嗎？

B: Of course, the more, the *merrier*.
當然囉！人越多越好！

💬 多多益善：

A: I have some boxes. Do you need them?
我有一些箱子，你需要它們嗎？

B: We are moving right now. So, yes, the more, the *merrier*.
我們現在正在搬家，所以越多越好囉！

* mer·ry	[ˈmɛrɪ]	形	快樂的

82. rub someone up the wrong way　惹惱某人

💬 個性使然：

A: How come nobody likes Sammy?
為什麼沒人喜歡珊咪？

B: It's because she rubs everyone up the wrong way.
因為她總是惹惱大家。

💬 做了讓人生氣的事情：

Oh no, I think I rub dad up the wrong way. He is really mad now!
糟了，我想我把爸爸給惹惱了，他現在真的很生氣了。

Chapter 02 人際社交 Interpersonal Relationships

83. It all *depends* on what one means by...
看某人對於……是指什麼意思

💬 **說得更明確一點：**

A: Could you lend me some money?
你可不可以借我一些錢？

B: It all *depends* on what you mean by "some."
看你「一些」指的是多少啊！

💬 **標準是什麼：**

A: Is it a difficult test?
這個考試難嗎？

B: It all *depends* on what you mean by "difficult."
看你「難」的定義是什麼囉！

* de·pend	[dɪˋpɛnd]	動	依賴、依靠

84. You are joking! (No kidding!) 別開玩笑了！

💬 **才不會信以為真：**

A: You are joking! I won't believe you.
別開玩笑了，我不會相信你的。

B: Hey, it's true.
嘿，這是真的。

💬 **信口開河：**

A: He says that he will give me a *mansion* if I marry him.
他說如果我嫁給他，他要給我一棟別墅。

B: You are joking! It's impossible.
別開玩笑了，那是不可能的。

💬 **正經一點：**

You are joking! It is not true.
別開玩笑了！這不是真的。

* man·sion	[ˋmænʃən]	名	宅邸、大廈

85. It's terrible.　糟透了。

💬 **電影不好看：**

A: How was the movie?
電影如何啊？

B: It was terrible.
糟透了。

💬 **早跟你說了不好吃：**

A: The food in the new restaurant was terrible.
新餐廳的食物很糟。

B: I told you so.
我跟你說過啦！

💬 **說謊不可取：**

It's terrible that she told a lie.
實在太糟糕了，她居然說謊了。

86. in one's book　在（某人）字典裡……；對……而言

💬 **不知緊張為何物：**

A: Aren't you *nervous* about singing on the stage for everyone?
你在臺上為大家唱歌不會覺得很緊張嗎？

B: There is no such thing as "*nervous*"in my book.
在我的字典裡沒有「緊張」這兩個字。

💬 **自以為是：**

Anyone who disagrees with him is wrong in his book.
對他而言，只要是不同意他的人都是錯的。

* nerv·ous	[ˈnɝvəs]	形	神經質的、膽怯的

87. I am *exhausted*.　我累翻了。

💬 **撐不下去了，休息一下：**

A: I need some rest. I am *exhausted*.
　　我需要休息一下，我累翻了。

B: We have only been walking for thirty minutes.
　　我們只走了三十分鐘。

💬 **再也沒有多餘的力氣了：**

A: Count me out. I am *exhausted*.
　　不要算我的份，我累翻了。

B: But we are short of one player.
　　可是我們少一個隊員。

💬 **筋疲力盡：**

I am exhausted because we walk all day long.
因為我們走了一整天，我真的好累。

* ex·haust	[ɪgˋzɔst]	動	耗盡

88. You ain't seen nothing yet!　你還沒看過更好（爛）的！

💬 **不止如此，還有更棒的呢：**

A: Wow! Did you see Karen's new ring? It is so big!
　　哇！你有沒有看到凱倫的新戒指？好大喔！

B: You ain't seen nothing yet! It's not her biggest ring.
　　你還沒看過更好的呢！那不是她最大的戒指。

💬 **不算最糟糕的：**

A: My car is like a big piece of *junk*.
　　我的車像是一塊大廢鐵！

B: You ain't seen nothing yet! Mine is already in the *junk* yard.
　　你還沒看過更爛的呢！我的車已經在廢車廠了！

* junk	[dʒʌŋk]	名	垃圾

89. to take a rain check　改天的邀請

💬 **不得已改期：**

As for going to the movies tonight, I will have to take a rain check.

抱歉，我今晚沒法跟你一起去看電影，我改天再邀你吧。

💬 **一定會加以補償的：**

About our date, I am afraid I will have to take a rain check.

我必須取消今晚的約會，但是我答應改天會再邀你。

🐱 Chat 不 斷 流

Heidi 海蒂	Jerry really rubs me up the wrong way! 傑瑞真的惹惱我了。
Doreen 朵琳	What's wrong? 發生什麼事？
Heidi 海蒂	He took my breakfast and ate it right in my face! 他搶走我的早餐，還在我面前把它吃掉。
Doreen 朵琳	Oh, you ain't seen nothing yet. One time, he took my watch and he didn't give it back until I said I was going to call the police! 你還沒看過更瞎的！有一次，他搶走我的手錶，直到我說要報警才還我！
Heidi 海蒂	You're joking. That's terrible! 真的假的，他真是糟透了！
Doreen 朵琳	We've all been through his horrible acts. 我們都領教過他的惡劣行徑。
Heidi 海蒂	He's a jerk in my book. 對我來說，他就是個混蛋。

Doreen 朵琳	I am exhausted just talking about him. 我罵他罵得累翻了。
Heidi 海蒂	Same. I might have to take a rain check on tonight's movie. 我也是，我們今晚看電影可能要改天再約。
Doreen 朵琳	That's alright. We can go to the movies some other day. 沒關係，我們可以改天再去看電影。

🎧 *Track 255*

90. **That's what friends are for.**　這才是好朋友啊！

💬 朋友之間理應如此：

A: Thank you for helping me out.
　　謝謝你幫我的忙！

B: Don't *mention* it! That's what friends are for.
　　別這麼說，這才是好朋友啊！

💬 義氣相挺：

A: You were very nice to lend me the money.
　　你真好，借我錢。

B: That's what friends are for.
　　這才是好朋友啊！

| * men·tion | [ˈmɛnʃən] | 動 | 提起 |

🎧 *Track 256*

91. **Let's get together next time.**　下次再約出來聚聚。

💬 這聚會真是太開心了：

A: Wow! What a night!
　　哇！今天晚上真棒！

B: Yeah! Let's get together next time.
　　對啊！我們下次再約出來聚聚！

💬 **巧遇寒暄：**

A: Let's get together next time.
下次再約出來聚聚！

B: Why not?
有何不可？

💬 **下一次再約吧：**

It's too late. Let's get together next time.
太晚了，下次再約出來聚聚。

🎧 *Track 257*

92. the tip of the *iceberg* 冰山的一角；危險的細微徵兆

💬 **還有更嚴重的：**

A: Could you believe that the criminals bribed the policeman?
你相不相信那些犯人賄賂了警察？

B: I think that's only the tip of the *iceberg*.
我覺得那只是冰山一角罷了！

💬 **只是一小部分而已：**

The *statistics* on abortion we know are only the tip of the iceberg.
我們所知道的墮胎統計數字只是冰山一角。

* ice·berg	[ˈaɪsˌbɝg]	名	冰山
* sta·tis·tic(s)	[stəˈtɪstɪk(s)]	名	統計值、統計量

🎧 *Track 258*

93. *behind* the scenes 在幕後；在黑暗中

💬 **勞苦功高的無名英雄：**

A: That movie was a great *success*!
那部電影相當成功！

B: A lot of people worked *behind* the scenes to make it happen.
許多幕後工作人員一起努力使它實現。

Chapter 02 人際社交 Interpersonal Relationships

💬 **另有其人：**

A: Isn't he the boss?
　　他不是老闆嗎？

B: Yup, but Harry is the boss *behind* the scenes.
　　是啊！可是哈利才是幕後的老闆。

* suc·cess	[sək`sɛs]	名	成功
* be·hind	[bɪ`haɪnd]	介	在……之後

🎧 *Track 259*

94. Speak of the *devil* (and he/she walks in).
說曹操，曹操到。

💬 **說人人就到：**

A: Janice called me last night.
　　詹妮斯昨天晚上打電話給我。

B: Speak of the *devil* and she walks in.
　　說曹操，曹操到。

💬 **同樣的情況：**

A: I heard Mary is getting a divorce.
　　我聽說瑪莉要離婚了。

B: Speak of the *devil* and she walks in. Why don't you ask her yourself.
　　說曹操，曹操到。你何不自己問她？

* dev·il	[`dɛvl̩]	名	魔鬼、惡魔

🎧 *Track 260*

95. right up/down someone's *alley*　某人的專長

💬 **善用個人長項：**

You can ask Jerry anything about cars. That's right up his *alley*.
你可以問傑利關於車的事情，那是他的專長。

術業有專攻：

You want to know about animals? Ask me! That's right down my *alley*.

你想知道關於動物的事情？問我！這是我的專長。

* al·ley	[ˈælɪ]	名	巷、小徑

🎧 *Track 261*

96. You never know what you can do *until* you try.
你不試試看，你不會知道自己的潛力。

不要妄自匪薄：

A: I don't think I can handle this project.
　　我想我無法處理這一項計畫。

B: You never know what you can do *until* you try.
　　你不試試看，你不會知道自己的潛力。

鼓勵他人勇於挑戰：

You should join the swim team! You never know what you can do *until* you try.

你應該要加入游泳隊的！你不試試看，你不會知道自己的潛力。

* un·til/till	[ənˈtɪl]/[tɪl]	連	直到……為止

🎧 *Track 262*

97. A penny saved is a penny *earned.*
存了一塊錢就是等於賺了一塊錢。

小氣財神：

A: Why are you so *stingy*?
　　你為什麼那麼小氣？

B: Don't you know? A penny saved is a penny *earned.*
　　你不知道嗎？存一塊錢就是賺了一塊錢！

省愈多，賺愈多：

Don't *waste* your money! A penny saved is a penny *earned.*
別浪費你的錢！存了一塊錢就是等於賺了一塊錢。

Chapter 02 人際社交 *Interpersonal Relationships*

141

* earn	[ɚn]	動	賺取、得到
* waste	[west]	動	浪費、濫用
* sting·y	[ˈstɪndʒɪ]	形	小氣的

🎧 *Track 263*

98. get/have cold feet　緊張

💬 壓力太大了：

A: Where is Judy? Is she ready yet?
茉莉在哪兒？她準備好了沒？

B: She is having cold feet. She needs a little time to herself.
她很緊張，她需要一些獨處的時間。

💭 欲臨陣脫逃：

I am having cold feet. I don't want to sing in front of everybody.
我好緊張喔！我不想在大家面前唱歌。

🎧 *Track 264*

99. set someone's sights on something
看好了某樣東西；決心要……

💬 已經看中意：

A: What kind of house are you thinking of buying?
你想買什麼樣的房子？

B: I have set my sights on that beach house.
我看上了那棟海邊的別墅。

💭 從小的志願：

A: When did you decide to become a *lawyer*?
你什麼時候決定要當一個律師的？

B: I have set my sights on it ever since I was a little girl.
當我還是一個小女孩時我就下定決心了。

* law·yer	[ˈlɔjɚ]	名	律師

🐱 Chat 不 斷 流

Lara 拉拉	I've set my sights on this management position. 我決定要去爭取這個管理職位。
Bill 比爾	What kind of company is that? 那是間什麼樣的公司？
Lara 拉拉	They make skin care products. 做護膚產品的。
Bill 比爾	Right up your alley! You should definitely go for it! 這就是妳的專長，妳一定要好好爭取！
Lara 拉拉	Yeah. Just hope I don't get cold feet right before the interview. 是啊，希望我在面試前不會突然很緊張。
Bill 比爾	Relax. You never know what you can do until you try. 放輕鬆，不試試看，妳不會知道自己的潛力。
Lara 拉拉	You're right. Thanks for helping me gain confidence. 說的沒錯，謝謝妳幫我建立信心。
Bill 比爾	Don't mention it. That's what friends are for! 小事一樁，這樣才是好朋友啊！
Lara 拉拉	Let's get together next time. 下次再約出來聚聚吧！
Bill 比爾	Sure thing! 一定的！

100. *Honesty* is the best *policy*. 誠實為上策。

💬 **不用擔心，說實話就對了：**

A: Do you think Chad will be angry if I tell him the truth?
如果我跟查德説實話，你覺得他會不會生氣？

B: No. *Honesty* is the best *policy*.
不會的，因為誠實為上策！

💭 **勸人誠實以對：**

You should tell the truth. *Honesty* is the best *policy*.
你應該説實話，因為誠實為上策！

| * hon·es·ty | [ˈɑnɪstɪ] | 名 | 正直、誠實 |
| * pol·i·cy | [ˈpɑləsɪ] | 名 | 政策 |

101. Some people never learn. 有些人總是學不乖。

💬 **惡習不改：**

A: Kevin got caught stealing again.
凱文又因為偷竊被抓了。

B: Some people never learn.
有些人就是學不乖。

💭 **白目沒藥醫：**

A: He had pissed her off by asking her weight once before, and he asked her again today.
他以前因為問她的體重惹她生氣，但他今天又問了一次！

B: Some people never learn.
有些人就是學不乖。

102. Beauty is only *skin* deep. 美麗是膚淺的。

💬 **自以為是：**

A: She thinks she is the most beautiful girl in her class.
她認為自己是班上最美的女生。

B: Well, she is pretty, but beauty is only *skin* deep.
她是很漂亮，但是美麗只是表面的。

💬 **內在美比外在美重要：**

You spent too much time putting on make-up. Remember, beauty is only *skin* deep.
你花太多時間化妝了，記住，美麗只是膚淺的。

* skin	[skɪn]	名	皮、皮膚

🎧 *Track 269*

103. Some people have all the luck.　有些人就是那麼幸運。

💬 **太令人羨慕了：**

A: Joe *married* the prettiest girl in school, who also happens to be the daughter of a millionaire.
喬和他學校裡最美的女生，也就是富豪的女兒結婚！

B: Some people have all the luck.
有些人就是那麼幸運！

💬 **人生一帆風順：**

Some people have all the luck. He has not only the greatest job, but also the happiest family.
有些人就是那麼幸運！他不但有一個很棒的工作，也有一個很快樂的家庭！

* mar·ry	[ˈmærɪ]	動	使結為夫妻、結婚

🎧 *Track 270*

104. Don't be such a *sore* loser.　不要輸不起。

💬 **怎麼可能：**

A: I can't believe I lost the game to you.
我無法相信我球賽輸給了你。

B: Don't be such a *sore* loser.
你真是輸不起！

Chapter 02 人際社交 *Interpersonal Relationships*

💬 **非贏不可：**

A: It's not fair! Let's start the game over.
　　不公平！我們重新再玩一次。

B: Don't be such a *sore* loser.
　　你真是輸不起！

* sore	[sor]	形	惹人反感的

🎧 *Track 271*

105. Never say die.　決不要灰心。

💬 **再撐一下，就快到了：**

A: I am never going to make it to the mountaintop.
　　我永遠爬不到山頂了啦！

B: Never say die. We are almost there.
　　決不要灰心，我們就快到了！

💬 **不會有事的：**

A: I don't think I could *bear* the *grief* anymore.
　　我想我再也不能忍受這傷心了。

B: Never say die. You will be OK.
　　決不要灰心，你會沒事的！

* bear	[bɛr]	動	忍受
* grief	[grif]	名	悲傷、感傷

🎧 *Track 272*

106. Seeing is believing.　眼見為憑；看到才算數。

💬 **親眼看見才算數：**

A: Do you know that Kerry bought a new Mercedece Benz?
　　你知不知道凱利買了一台新的賓士？

B: Seeing is believing. Let's go check it out.
　　眼見為憑！我們去看看吧！

💬 **相信自己所見：**

A: Why don't you believe me?
　　你為什麼不相信我？

B: Seeing is believing. I will have to see it with my own eyes.
　　眼見為憑，我得用我自己的眼睛看到。

🎧 *Track 273*

107. **Do you have a second now?**　你現在有時間嗎？

💬 **詢問對方有空嗎？：**

A: Do you have a second now?
　　你現在有時間嗎？

B: Yes, I do.　有。

💬 **同樣的意思：**

A: Do you have a second now?
　　你現在有時間嗎？

B: Sure.　當然。

🎧 *Track 274*

108. *Drop* in sometime!　有空來坐坐。

💬 **告別時：**

A: Bye! See you next time.
　　再見！下次見！

B: Remember to *drop* in sometime.
　　記得有空來坐坐喔！

💬 **歡迎你隨時來哦：**

A: My house is just over there. You can *drop* in sometime.
　　我家就在那，你有空可以來坐坐。

B: Sure, I will.
　　當然，我會的。

💬 **邀約：**

Please *drop* in sometime!
有空請來坐坐。

| * drop | [drɑp] | 動 | 掉下 |

109. next time 下次吧

💬 **一定會再來：**

A: When will you come?
　　你什麼時候會再來？

B: Next time.
　　下次吧！

💬 **同樣的情形：**

A: When will I see you again?
　　我什麼時候才能再見到你？

B: Next time.
　　下次吧！

💬 **也可以這樣說：**

Come see me next time.
下次來看看我吧。

😺 Chat 不 斷 流

Michelle 蜜雪兒	Do you have a second now? 你現在有時間嗎？
Lily 莉莉	Sure, what's up? 當然，怎麼了？
Michelle 蜜雪兒	Can't believe that I have lost the singing contest. 真不敢相信我輸了歌唱比賽。
Lily 莉莉	Sorry to hear that. 我很遺憾。
Michelle 蜜雪兒	Some people have all the luck. I bet she won just because she's prettier! 有些人就是那麼幸運，她一定只是因為比我漂亮才贏的。

Lily	Hey, don't be such a sore loser. Beauty is only skin deep. She must have performed well. 不要輸不起了，美麗是膚淺的，她獲選一定是因為表現不錯。
Michelle 蜜雪兒	I am so disappointed in myself. I'll never succeed! 我對自己好失望，我一輩子都不會成功！
Lily 莉莉	Never say die! I'm sure you'll do better next time. 決不要灰心！我相信你下次會表現更好的。
Michelle 蜜雪兒	Alright. Thanks for cheering me up. 好吧，謝謝你的鼓勵。
Lily 莉莉	Drop in at my place! 來我家坐坐吧。
Michelle 蜜雪兒	Thanks, I will, but maybe next time. 謝謝，我會的，也許下次。

🎧 *Track 277*

110. **Same to you.** 你也一樣。

💬 **祝福你：**

A: Have a nice day.
祝你今天愉快。

B: Same to you.
你也是喔！

💭 **也可以這樣用：**

A: Have a nice weekend.
祝你周末愉快！

B: Same to you.
你也是喔！

111. **The feeling is** *mutual*.　有同感。

💬 心有戚戚焉：

A: It is a pleasure to talk to you.
　　和你說話真的很開心。

B: The feeling is *mutual*.
　　我有同感耶！

💬 英雄所見略同：

A: I don't like the new girl in our class.
　　我不喜歡我們班上新來的女同學。

B: The feeling is *mutual*.
　　我有同感。

* mu·tu·al	[ˈmjutʃʊəl]	形	相互的、共同的

112. **the** *calm* **before the** *storm*　暴風雨前的寧靜

💬 山風欲來之勢：

A: Everything seemed well at the party.
　　派對感覺上一切都很好啊！

B: It's the *calm* before the *storm*.
　　這是暴風雨前的寧靜。

💬 同樣的情形：

A: Perry seemed to be rather quiet at dinner.
　　派利晚餐的時候顯得特別安靜。

B: It's the *calm* before the *storm*.
　　這是暴風雨前的寧靜。

* storm	[stɔrm]	名	風暴
* calm	[kɑm]	形	平靜的

113. **Every dog has his day.**
人人皆有得意的一天；十年風水輪流轉。

💬 意氣風發：

A: You seem happy today.
你今天看起來很開心嘛！

B: Every dog has his day.
人人皆有得意的一天囉！

💬 幸運從天而降：

A: Congratulations! You won the *lottery*.
恭喜！你贏了彩券。

B: Every dog has his day.
人人皆有得意的一天囉！

* lot·ter·y	[ˈlɑtərɪ]	名	彩券、樂透

114. **A good man is hard to find.**　好人難找。

💬 終於找到人了：

A: Do you think Danny is *suitable* for the job?
你覺得丹尼適合這個工作嗎？

B: He seems to be nice. A good man is hard to find nowadays.
他似乎人很好，現在好人難找啊！

💬 緣份，可遇不可求：

A: Why don't you get married?
你為什麼不結婚？

B: A good man is hard to find.
好男人難找啊！

* suit·a·ble	[ˈsutəbl]	形	適合的

Chapter 02 人際社交 Interpersonal Relationships

115. sell like hot cakes　很暢銷

💬 銷售成績很好：

A: How is the sales *figure* on your new album?
你的新專輯賣得怎麼樣？

B: It is selling like hot cakes.
賣得很好。

💬 反應很熱烈：

A: Sarah's book sold like hot cakes.
莎拉的書賣得很好！

B: I know, I heard a lot of people talking about it.
我知道啊，我聽到別人都在說呢！

* fig·ure	[ˈfɪgjɚ]	名	數字、人影

116. Easy come, easy go.　來得快，去得快。

💬 橫財總是留不住：

A: I lost all the money I won from the lottery.
我把買彩券贏來的錢都輸光了。

B: Well, easy come, easy go.
來得快，去得也快。

💬 不勞而獲：

A: My friend gave me some free tickets to the movies, but I lost them.
我朋友給了我一些免費的電影票，可是我把它們弄丟了。

B: Easy come, easy go.
來得快，去得也快囉！

117.*Practice* makes perfect.　熟能生巧。

💬 不斷練習才能精進：

A: I have been *practicing* playing the piano the whole morning.
我已經練鋼琴練了一早上了。

B: Practice makes perfect. Your efforts will all pay off.
熟能生巧！你的努力會有代價的。

💬 好還要更好：

A: Why are you still working on your backhand *swing*?
你怎麼還在練你的反手拍？

B: Practice makes perfect! I want to be a real pro.
熟能生巧，我要當一個真正的職業選手。

* swing	[swɪŋ]	動	搖動
* prac·tice	['præktɪs]	動	練習

118.drive someone to the wall
使某人發瘋／受不了；使某人束手無策

💬 安靜點！我在念書：

A: Quit playing the guitar. You are driving me to the wall. I am studying.
別再彈吉他了，你快把我逼瘋了！我在讀書。

B: I am sorry. I didn't know you were studying.
對不起，我不知道你在讀書。

💬 別再煩我了：

Don't ask me any more questions. You are driving me to the wall.
別再問我問題了，你快把我逼瘋了！

119. get something off one's chest
傾吐心中的事；落下心中的大石

💬 **想要一吐為快：**

A: What's wrong with you?
你怎麼了？

B: Could I talk to you for a minute? I really have to get this off my chest.
我可以跟你談一下嗎？我必須跟你傾吐心中的這件事。

💬 **終於安心了：**

Thanks for telling me the truth. I finally got it off my chest.
謝謝你跟我說實話，我終於落下心中的大石了。

🐱 Chat 不斷流

Bailey 貝莉	I have to get something off my chest. 有些話我想說，但忍了很久。
Amanda 亞曼達	Sure, what's going on? 說吧，怎麼了？
Bailey 貝莉	Sara's shoes are everywhere. It's really driven me to the wall! 莎拉的鞋丟得家裡亂七八糟，快把我逼瘋了！
Amanda 亞曼達	Oh, trust me. The feeling is mutual. 相信我，我也有同感。
Bailey 貝莉	I wish we could just kick her out of the house. 真希望我們能把她趕出去。
Amanda 亞曼達	Come on. Sara is messy and loud, but she isn't that bad of a person. 別這樣嘛，莎拉或許髒又吵，但她個性不差。

Bailey 貝莉	You're right. A good roommate is hard to find. 說得對，好室友是很難找的。
Amanda 亞曼達	Have you tried the face masks from that shop around the corner? 你試過轉角那家店的面膜嗎？
Bailey 貝莉	No I haven't. Those things sell like hot cakes! 我還沒，那些面膜很暢銷。
Amanda 亞曼達	I was lucky enough to get some. They're in the fridge 我很幸運搶到幾個，放在冰箱裡。.
Bailey 貝莉	Should we put on the face masks and watch a movie before Sara gets back, to enjoy the calm before the storm together? 我們要不要邊敷面膜，邊看電影，在莎拉回家前一起享受暴風雨前的寧靜？
Amanda 亞曼達	That sounds great. 聽起來很棒。
Bailey 貝莉	You're the best friend anyone could ever ask for. 你是世上最棒的朋友！
Amanda 亞曼達	Same to you! 你也是！

🎧 *Track 288*

120. Two wrongs don't make a right.
兩個錯誤不等於一個正確；報復於事無補。

💬 **冤冤相報何時了：**

A: Jill is always talking behind my back, so I am going to do the same to her.
吉兒每次都在我背後說我壞話，所以我也要這樣做。

B: Two wrongs don't make a right.
報復於事無補。

A: He always takes the bus without paying the fees. Why shouldn't I?
他搭公車總是不付錢，我為什麼不也這樣？

B: Two wrongs don't make a right. Besides, he will get caught someday.
兩個錯誤不等於一個正確，再說他有一天會被抓到的。

🎧 *Track 289*

121. the *blind* leading the *blind*　外行教外行

💭 我一點也不內行：

A: Could you tell me how to fix this *machine*?
你可不可以告訴我怎麼修理這個機器？

B: That will be the *blind* leading the *blind* since I know nothing about *machines*.
那根本是外行教外行，因為我對機器一竅不通。

💬 半斤八兩：

A: When we go to Japan, you will be our tour guide.
我們到日本的時候，你要當我們的導遊。

B: That will be the *blind* leading the *blind*.
那根本是外行帶著外行。

* blind	[blaɪnd]	形	瞎的
* ma·chine	[məˈʃin]	名	機器、機械

🎧 *Track 290*

122. *Appearances* can be *deceiving.*
外表是會騙人的（外表看不出來）。

💭 遇人不淑：

A: I thought that he was a great guy until he dumped Mary.
我一直以為他是一個好人，直到他甩了瑪莉。

B: Well, *appearances* can be *deceiving*.
外表是會騙人的。

He didn't look like such a good leader. I guess, *appearances* can be *deceiving*.

他看起來不像一個這麼棒的領導者，我想外表是看不出來的。

* ap·pear·ance	[ə`pɪrəns]	名	出現、露面
* de·ceive	[dɪ`siv]	動	欺詐、詐騙

🎧 *Track 291*

123. Don't put all your eggs in one basket.
別把所有雞蛋放在同一個籃子裡；別孤注一擲。

投資要分散風險：

A: I am going to *invest* all my money in stocks.
　　我將要把我所有的錢投資股票。

B: Don't put all your eggs in one basket.
　　別把所有雞蛋放在同一個籃子裡。

同樣的意思：

A: I am not going to *apply* for any other school except Harvard.
　　哈佛以外的學校我都不會申請。

B: Don't put all your eggs in one basket.
　　別把所有雞蛋放在同一個籃子裡。

* in·vest	[ɪn`vɛst]	動	投資
* ap·ply	[ə`plaɪ]	動	請求、應用

🎧 *Track 292*

124. You can't please everyone.
你無法使每一個人都滿意；你無法討好每一個人。

每個人喜好都不一樣：

A: Everyone loved the cake I baked except Judy.
　　除了茱蒂以外，每一個人都喜歡我烤的蛋糕。

B: You can't please everyone.
　　你無法使每一個人都滿意。

💬 **總是有人特別挑剔：**

A: Jim complained that the soup was too salty.
吉姆抱怨說湯太鹹了。

B: You can't please everyone. Besides, he is really picky.
你無法使每一個人都滿意，再說他真的很挑。

🎧 *Track 293*

125. An eye for an eye (and a tooth for a tooth).
以眼還眼，以牙還牙。

💬 **以暴制暴是對的嗎：**

A: I think the death penalty is fair. An eye for an eye and a tooth for a tooth.
我覺得死刑是公平的。所謂以眼還眼，以牙還牙。

B: I think death penalty is *barbarian*.
我覺得死刑很野蠻。

💬 **君子報仇三年不晚：**

An eye for an eye and a tooth for a tooth. I am going to take *revenge*, just wait and see.
以眼還眼，以牙還牙，我要報復。你等著看吧！

* re·venge	[rɪˋvɛndʒ]	名	報復
* bar·bar·i·an	[barˋberɪən]	名	野蠻的

🎧 *Track 294*

126. Let me have it! / Let's have it!　告訴我（們）怎麼一回事？

💬 **八卦人人愛：**

A: Well, I saw Mr. Wang going to the movies with Kelly last night.
我昨天晚上看到王先生跟凱莉一起去看電影。

B: Let me have it! What else did you see?
告訴我，你還看到了什麼？

💬 **好想趕快知道啊：**

A: Now! I am going to *announce* the winner of this *contest*.
我現在要宣佈這一次比賽的得獎者。

B: Let's have it! I wonder who will be the winner this year.
告訴我們吧！不知道今年誰會得獎。

💬 集思廣益：

Let's have it. We can find a *solution* together.
告訴我們吧！我們可以一起想辦法。

* an·nounce	[ə`naʊns]	動	宣告、公佈、通知
* con·test	[`kɑntɛst]	名	比賽
* so·lu·tion	[sə`luʃən]	名	解決、解釋、溶解

🎧 *Track 295*

127. cost someone an arm and a leg　花大筆錢

💬 原來你這麼有錢啊：

A: It cost me an arm and a leg to buy this boat.
我花了許多錢買這艘船。

B: I never knew you were so rich.
我從來不知道你這麼有錢。

💬 耗費鉅資：

It must cost her an arm and a leg to buy the new house.
她買那棟新房子一定花了一大筆錢！

🎧 *Track 296*

128. have the *upper* hand　占優勢

💬 後繼無力：

A: So you lost the basketball game?
所以你們籃球比賽輸了？

B: We have the *upper* hand at the beginning of the game, but we lost it in the end.
比賽一開始我們是占優勢，但我們最後還是輸了。

💬 主領導位置：

They have the *upper* hand in this lawsuit.
他們在這宗訴訟案占優勢。

* up·per	[`ʌpɚ]	副	在上位

129. nothing to write home about
沒什麼值得說的；不值得推薦的

💬 **乏善可陳：**

A: So how was that movie?
那電影怎樣？

B: It is nothing to write home about.
它實在是沒什麼值得說的。

💭 **沒有任何優點：**

That Japanese restaurant is certainly nothing to write home about. The food was really bad.
那個日本餐廳實在是不值得推薦，食物真是不好吃。

🗣 Chat 不 斷 流

Jessica 潔西卡	How's the new girl? 新來的女孩怎麼樣？
Randy 蘭迪	I don't know why I'm training her! This is totally the blind leading the blind! 我不懂我為什麼在訓練她！這根本是外行教外行！
Jessica 潔西卡	Is she alright at least? 至少她還行嗎？
Randy 蘭迪	I thought she looked clever, but man, I think appearances can be deceiving! 我以為她看起來很聰明，但老兄，我覺得外表是會騙人的！
Jessica 潔西卡	Oh, is she that bad? 她有這麼糟啊？
Randy 蘭迪	Yeah. There is also something that I need to tell you about... 對啊，我還要跟你說一件事……

Jessica 潔西卡	What? 什麼事？
Randy 蘭迪	I'm afraid you won't like it. 恐怕你不會喜歡這件事。
Jessica 潔西卡	Oh, let me have it! 告訴我怎麼一回事吧！
Randy 蘭迪	She broke two of your antique lamps within the first ten minutes. 她剛開始工作十分鐘，就毀了兩盞古董檯燈。
Jessica 潔西卡	No way! Those things cost me an arm and a leg. She's going to have to pay me back! 不會吧！那些檯燈可花了我大筆的錢，她必須賠償我！
Randy 蘭迪	Oh, come on. She won't be able to afford those things. 拜託，她買不起那些東西的。
Jessica 潔西卡	Or I'm going to break her arms! An eye for an eye and a tooth for a tooth! 不然我就要打斷她的手，以牙還牙，以眼還眼！
Randy 蘭迪	Calm down! Two wrongs don't make a right. 冷靜！報復於事無補。

🎧 *Track 299*

130. packed in like sardines　擠得要命（人很多）

💬 <u>像擠沙丁魚一樣：</u>

A: It's a pain in the neck taking a bus during rush hours.
在尖峰時間搭公車真的很討厭。

B: Yup, the passengers in the bus are packed in like sardines.
是啊！公車裡的乘客都擠得要命。

💬 <u>摩肩接踵：</u>

We went to the club last night, and the people there were packed in like sardines.
我們昨晚去夜店跳舞，那裡的人真多。

* pack	[pæk]	動	擠進、塞滿
* sar·dine	[sɑrˋdin]	名	沙丁魚

🎧 *Track 300*

131. come out smelling like a rose　一枝獨秀

💬 脫穎而出：

A: How did James do on his exam?
　　詹姆斯考得如何？

B: Everybody else did okay, but he came out smelling like a rose.
　　其他人考得都還好，而他卻一枝獨秀！

💬 技高一籌，獨占鰲頭：

All my hard work has finally paid off. My work comes out smelling like a rose in the fair.
我的所有辛苦終於有代價了，我的作品在展覽會上一枝獨秀。

🎧 *Track 301*

132. hear through the *grapevine*　聽到謠傳

💬 人們很容易道聽塗說：

A: Where did you hear such a thing?
　　你從哪聽來的這件事啊？

B: I heard through the *grapevine*.
　　我聽別人說的。

💬 聽到風聲了：

I heard through the grapevine that she is getting married.
我聽說她要結婚了。

* grape·vine	[ˋgrepˏvaɪn]	名	消息來源；葡萄藤

133. **What's it got to do with you?**　干你什麼事？

💬 別多管閒事：

A: Go ahead and do it.
去做！

B: What's it got to do with you?
干你什麼事！

💬 不要你管：

A: Don't be mad at him anymore.
不要再生他的氣了！

B: What's it got to do with you?
干你什麼事！

134. **read you *loud* and *clear***　聽得很清楚；很了解你

💬 聽得清楚明白：

A: Can you hear me?
你聽得到我說話嗎？

B: Yes, I read you *loud* and *clear*.
可以，我聽得很清楚。

💬 我懂了：

I know what you mean. I read you *loud* and *clear*.
我知道你的意思，我很了解你。

* loud	[laʊd]	形	大聲的、響亮的
* clear	[klɪr]	形	清楚的、明確的

Chapter 02 人際社交 Interpersonal Relationships

135. have a sweet tooth　喜歡甜食（喜好某物）

💬 **無甜不歡：**

A: I have a sweet tooth. I can't *resist* chocolate.
　　我喜歡吃甜食，我不能抗拒巧克力。

B: Me, too.
　　我也是。

💬 **也可以這樣說：**

She has a sweet tooth. She loves chocolate cakes best.
她喜歡吃甜食，她最愛巧克力蛋糕了。

* re·sist	[rɪˈzɪst]	動	抵抗

136. **I am fine.** / **It couldn't be better.**　我很好；再好不過了。

💬 **熱情回應：**

A: How are you?
　　你好嗎？

B: I am fine, thank you .
　　我很好，謝謝。

💬 **沒有比現在更好的了：**

A: How are you? You look really happy.
　　你好嗎？你看起來很開心。

B: It couldn't be better! I am getting married next month.
　　我再好不過了。我下個月就要結婚了。

💬 **一切都沒有問題：**

I am fine living alone.
我一個人住很好。

137. Maybe.　說不定……

💬 也許哦：

A: Is it going to rain?
會下雨嗎？

B: Maybe.
說不定會……

💬 不一定耶：

A: Are you going?
你會去嗎？

B: Maybe.
說不定會……

💬 下次再說吧：

Maybe we can *discuss* this next time.
或許我們可以下次再討論。

| * dis·cuss | [dɪˈskʌs] | 動 | 討論、商議 |

138. Are you ready?　準備好了嗎？

💬 準備好了就出發：

A: Are you ready?
準備好了嗎？

B: Yes, let's go.
好了，走吧！

💬 再給一點時間：

A: Are you ready?
準備好了嗎？

B: Can you wait for me?
你可以等我嗎？

Chapter 02 人際社交 Interpersonal Relationships

165

139. know someone like the back of one's hand　很了解某人

💬 **真有默契：**

A: How do you know I want a music box?
　　你怎麼知道我想要一個音樂盒？

B: I know you like the back of my hand.
　　我很了解你啊！

💭 **不可能會這麼做：**

I know my son like the back of my hand. He would never steal.
我很了解我的兒子，他絕對不會偷東西的。

🐼 Chat 不 斷 流

Ben 班恩	I heard through the grapevine that you broke up with Wayne. 我聽到謠傳說你跟韋恩分手了。
Kelly 凱莉	Yeah. It's true. 是真的。
Ben 班恩	Are you alright? 你還好嗎？
Kelly 凱莉	Couldn't be better! 再好不過了！
Ben 班恩	Come on, I know you like the back of my hand. You must be devastated. 少來了，我很了解你，你一定難過極了。
Kelly 凱莉	Maybe we will get back together someday. 也許我們有一天會復合。
Ben 班恩	Don't be silly. 別傻了。

Kelly 凱莉	What's it got to do with you? 干你什麼事？
Ben 班恩	I just don't want you to do something that you'd regret later! 我只是不想讓你做會後悔的事。
Kelly 凱莉	Alright, thanks. 好吧，謝謝你。
Ben 班恩	Chocolate? 來點巧克力？
Kelly 凱莉	Sure. You know I've always had a sweet tooth! 當然好，你也知道我一直都愛甜食。

🎧 *Track 310*

140. come away empty-handed   一無所獲；沒買

💬 **太貴了，什麼都沒有買：**

A: Did you get anything in that shop?
你在那店裡有沒有買東西？

B: I came away empty-handed since everything there was too expensive.
我什麼都沒買，店裡的東西太貴了！

💭 **空手而回：**

I came away *empty*-handed from the *auction*. The *antiques* cost more than I can afford.
我在那拍賣場什麼都沒有買，那些古董都太貴了！

* emp·ty	[ˋɛmptɪ]	形	空的
* auc·tion	[ˋɔkʃən]	名	拍賣
* an·tique	[ænˋtik]	名	古玩、古董

141. put / lay... on the line   坦白的說；冒……風險

💬 **坦白從寬：**

A: Put it on the line, Sylvia. Did you *spread* the *rumor*?
席維亞，妳坦白的說吧，是妳散播謠言的嗎？

B: Yes, I *admit* it.
是的，我承認是我說的。

💬 **勇氣過人：**

A: He put his life on the line to save that boy.
他冒著生命危險去救那個小男孩。

B: What a man!
了不起的男人！

* spread	[sprɛd]	動	展開、傳布
* ru·mor	[ˈrumɚ]	名	謠言
* ad·mit	[ədˈmɪt]	動	承認

142. like a fish out of water   像離開水的魚；感到尷尬不適應

💬 **會不會不自在：**

A: You must feel like a fish out of water in our women's gathering, Peter.
彼特，你在我們女人的聚會中一定覺得很尷尬！

B: No, it's my pleasure.
不會，這是我的榮幸。

💬 **太難為情了：**

I felt like a fish out of water when I found that I wore different socks to work.
當我發現我穿著兩隻不同的襪子上班，我覺得好尷尬。

143. It's very *dangerous...* ·······真危險

💬 太危險了：

A: It's very *dangerous* to go into that forest at night.
晚上進去那森林真危險。

B: Why? Is it *haunted*?
為什麼？有鬼嗎？

💬 小心為上：

A: Don't put the knife there. It's very *dangerous*.
別把刀放那裡，很危險。

B: Sorry.
對不起。

💬 千萬不要冒險：

It's very dangerous to walk alone at night.
一個人走夜路很危險。

| * dan·ger·ous | [ˈdendʒərəs] | 形 | 危險的 |
| * haunted | [ˈhɔntɪd] | 形 | 鬧鬼的 |

144. The first step is always the hardest. 萬事起頭難。

💬 開始就成功一半：

A: I don't think I am ever going to make it.
我想我絕不會成功的。

B: The first step is always the hardest. Don't *quit* now.
萬事起頭難，現在別放棄。

💬 頭過身就過：

A: French is so hard! I am having so much trouble.
法文真難！我遇到好多困難。

B: Don't worry! The first step is always the hardest.
別擔心！萬事起頭難。

| * quit | [kwɪt] | 動 | 離去、解除 |

145. Times change, people change. 時間會變，人也會變。

💬 人不可同日而語：

A: I thought Lisa was the most *conservative* person on earth, but look at her now.
我以為莉莎是全世界最保守的人，可是現在你看看她。

B: Times change, people change.
時間會變，人也會變。

💬 不同階段有不同想法：

A: When I was young, I wanted to be a teacher.
我小時候想當一個老師。

B: Times change, people change.
時間會變，人也會變。

* con·ser·va·tive	[kənˋsəvətɪv]	形	保守的、保守黨的

146. Birds of a *feather flock* together. 物以類聚。

💬 近朱者赤近墨者黑：

A: John and his friends have all pierced their ears.
約翰和他朋友們都穿耳洞了。

B: Birds of a *feather flock* together.
物以類聚啊！

💬 氣味相投：

A: Wow! You are also a fan of Michael Jackson.
哇！你也是麥可傑克森的歌迷！

B: We are best friends. Birds of a *feather flock* together.
我們是最好的朋友，物以類聚囉！

* feath·er	[ˋfɛðɚ]	名	羽毛、裝飾
* flock	[flɑk]	名	禽群、人群

147. **Give someone an inch and he'll take a mile.** 得寸進尺。

💬 太過分了：

A: I let Susan *borrow* my car for a day, but she kept it for a week.
我的車借給蘇珊一天，但她卻借了一個禮拜。

B: You give her an inch, and she'll take a mile.
有些人就是得寸進尺。

💭 得了便宜還賣乖：

A: She never returned the money that I lent her. Now she is asking for more.
她從來沒把我的錢還我，現在她還想要更多。

B: You give her an inch, and she'll take a mile.
有些人就是得寸進尺！

* bor·row	[ˋbɑro]	動	借來、採用

148. **Don't press your luck.** 不要得寸進尺。

💬 也太貪得無厭了：

A: Could you *lend* me $500 more?
你可不可以再借我 $500 ？

B: Don't press your luck.
你不要得寸進尺。

💭 要適可而止：

A: May I stay in your house and use your car this summer?
我這個夏天可以住在你家並開你的車嗎？

B: Don't press your luck. You should be *grateful* that I let you stay in my house.
你不要得寸進尺。我讓你住在我家你就應該覺得慶幸了。

* lend	[lɛnd]	動	借出
* grate·ful	[ˋgretfəl]	形	感激的、感謝的

149. (That's) fair enough.　這樣很合理

💬 一人一半：

A: Let's share the money fifty-fifty.
這些錢我們各分一半。

B: That's fair enough.
這樣很合理！

🗨 分工合作：

A: Why don't you take out the trash and I do the *laundry*?
不如你倒垃圾，我洗衣服。

B: That sounds fair enough.
聽起來很合理啊！

* laun·dry	[ˈlɔndrɪ]	名	洗衣店、送洗的衣服

🐾 Chat 不斷流

Fred 弗萊德	Brian, I think I want out of this business. 布萊恩，我想退出公司。
Brian 布萊恩	How come? 為什麼？
Fred 弗萊德	I feel like a fish out of water. Maybe I should go back to an office job. 我覺得自己好像離開水的魚，也許我該回到上班族的生活。
Brian 布萊恩	The first step is always the hardest. We've already been through the hardest part! 萬事起頭難，我們已經解決最困難的部份了！
Fred 弗萊德	I just don't want to end up coming away empty-handed, and going home without much money left. 我只是不想一無所穫，最後口袋空空。

Brian 布萊恩	I've put myself on the line for our business. Now you want to quit? 我為這個事業承擔所有風險，現在你居然想退出？
Fred 弗萊德	I'm really sorry about this. 我很抱歉。
Brian 布萊恩	You better think again. 你最好三思。
Fred 弗萊德	Times change, people change. This is not what I want anymore. 時間會變，人也會變，這已經不是我想要的了。
Brian 布萊恩	What do you want then? 那你想要什麼？
Fred 弗萊德	Just a steady job, so I can make enough money to feed my wife and kids. 一份穩定的工作，好讓我賺足夠的錢養活妻小。
Brian 布萊恩	Fair enough. 這倒是很合理。
Fred 弗萊德	Maybe when you make money, I will come back. 也許等你賺大錢，我會再回公司。
Brian 布萊恩	Don't press your luck. 別得寸進尺。

🎧 *Track 321*

150. along the way 順便

💬 **請他人順便幫忙：**

A: Will you take this along the way home?
你可以順便把這個帶回家嗎？

B: Sure.
當然。

A: Will you buy some drinks along the way?
你可以順便買些飲料嗎？

B: No problem.
沒問題。

剛好順路趁便：

I bought a cake along the way.
我順路買了個蛋糕。

🎧 *Track 322*

151. stand the test of time   接受時間的考驗

時間是最好的證明：

A: There are a lot of new coffee shops *around* this *area*.
這附近有很多新的咖啡店。

B: Only a few will stand the test of time.
只有一些可以經得過時間的考驗。

已經通過測試：

A: Why don't you buy a new car?
你為什麼不買一部新車？

B: My old car has stood the test of time. I don't want to part with it.
因為我的老爺車已經通過時間的考驗，我不想跟它分開了。

* a·round	[əˋraʊnd]	副	大約、在周圍
* ar·e·a	[ˋɛrɪə]	名	地區、領域

🎧 *Track 323*

152. a bed of roses   稱心如意的生活

世事總不盡如人意：

A: I really want to live in the *mountains* like you.
我真想跟你一樣住在高山上。

B: Life is not a bed of roses in the winter.
冬天並不好受。

A: Do you enjoy being a student?
你喜歡當學生嗎？

B: *Compared* to working, being a student is like a bed of roses.
和工作比起來，當學生真的是很棒的生活。

* moun·tain	[ˈmauntn̩]	名	高山
* comp·are	[kəmˈpɛr]	動	比較

🎧 *Track 324*

153. Achilles' heel　一個人的弱點

💬 美中不足：

A: She writes great stories.
她寫的故事很棒。

B: Her Achilles' heel is that she can't type very fast.
但她的弱點是她打字沒辦法打很快。

💬 人沒有十全十美：

A: John can surely run!
約翰真會跑哪！

B: His Achilles' heel is that he always gets *nervous* in the race.
但他的弱點是他在比賽中總是會緊張。

* nerv·ous	[ˈnɝvəs]	形	神經質的、膽怯的

🎧 *Track 325*

154. go the *distance*　堅持到底；完成全部

💬 下定決心：

A: Do you think you can go the *distance*?
你覺得你可以堅持到底嗎？

B: I'm *determined* to finish this project.
我已經決心要完成這個計畫。

Chapter 02 人際社交 *Interpersonal Relationships*

175

💬 **奮戰不懈：**

A: We lost the game, but we went the *distance* to the finals.
我們比賽輸了，但是我們一直堅持到最後的決賽。

B: I really *admire* your *spirit*.
我真的很欣賞你們的精神。

* dis·tance	[ˈdɪstəns]	名	距離
* de·ter·mine	[dɪˈtɜmɪn]	動	決定
* ad·mire	[ədˈmaɪr]	動	欽佩、讚賞
* spir·it	[ˈspɪrɪt]	名	精神

🎧 *Track 326*

155. water under the *bridge*　過去式；無法挽回的過去

💬 **過去的就讓它過去吧：**

A: I want to apologize for fighting with you in high school.
我想要為我高中時跟你打架的事向你道歉。

B: Forget about it. It was all water under the *bridge*.
算了吧，那已經是很久以前的事了。

💬 **機會稍縱即逝：**

My only chance of *promoting* is water under the *bridge*.
我唯一的升遷機會已經成過去式了。

* bridge	[brɪdʒ]	名	橋
* pro·mote	[prəˈmot]	動	晉升

🎧 *Track 327*

156. Monkey see, monkey do.　有樣學樣。

💬 **學習從模仿開始：**

A: My little sister saw me putting on my lipstick, so she did the same.
我妹妹看到我擦口紅，她也那麼做。

B: Monkey see, monkey do.
有樣學樣！

流行一窩風：

A: Why did your brother pierce his ears?
你弟弟幹嘛穿耳洞？

B: His friends all did the same. I guess monkey see, monkey do.
他的朋友也都這麼做，這是有樣學樣。

🎧 *Track 328*

157. **Different strokes for different folks.** 人各有所好。

尊重他人的言行：

A: She looks so funny in that hat!
她戴那頂帽子看起真好笑！

B: Don't laugh at her. Different strokes for different folks.
別笑她，人各有所好！

同樣的意思：

A: Did you see what John wore to the party? I don't know how he could stand a floral shirt!
你有沒有看到約翰穿去派對的衣服？我不知道他怎麼可以忍受一件花襯衫！

B: Different strokes for different folks.
人各有所好！

* stroke	[strok]	名	打擊、筆畫

🎧 *Track 329*

158. **Every family has a *skeleton* in the closet.**
家家有本難念的經。

沒什麼好說的：

A: Can you tell me about your family?
你可不可以跟我說說你的事？

B: I don't want to talk about it. Every family has a *skeleton* in the closet.
我不想說，家家有本難念的經。

A: I didn't know that Mary had to work to pay her *tuition*.
我不知道瑪莉得工作來賺她的學費。

B: Her dad was a drunk. Every family has a *skeleton* in the closet.
她爸爸是個酒鬼，家家有本難念的經。

* skel·e·ton	[ˈskɛlətn̩]	名	骨骼、骨架
* tu·i·tion	[tjuˈɪʃən]	名	學費

🎧 *Track 330*

159. I'll *accompany* you. 我陪你。

你不孤單：

A: I'll be so *lonely* here.
我在這裡會很寂寞。

B: I'll *accompany* you.
我陪你。

一同前往：

A: I don't want to go *alone*.
我不要自己去。

B: I'll accompany you.
我陪你。

陪伴左右：

I'll *accompany* you to the hospital.
我陪你到醫院。

* ac·com·pa·ny	[əˈkʌmpənɪ]	動	隨行、陪伴、伴隨
* lone·ly	[ˈlonlɪ]	形	孤單的、寂寞的
* a·lone	[əˈlon]	形	單獨的

🐱 Chat 不斷流

Brittany 布蘭妮	Hey Jamie. I got you a bar of chocolate along the way. 嘿，傑米，我在路上買了一條巧克力給你。
Jamie 傑米	Thanks! 謝謝！
Brittany 布蘭妮	How's the chocolate? 巧克力好吃嗎？
Jamie 傑米	I don't really like it. 我不太喜歡。
Brittany 布蘭妮	That's a shame. Well, different strokes for different folks! 真可惜，但人各有所好。
Jamie 傑米	Exactly. 沒錯。
Brittany 布蘭妮	How's it going? 最近怎麼樣？
Jamie 傑米	Not great. I tried to go the distance with Amy, but still our relationship didn't stand the test of time. She broke up with me. 我不好，我試著和艾咪堅持到底，但我們的愛情依然經不起時間的考驗，她跟我分手了。
Brittany 布蘭妮	Now you know, life is not a bed of roses. 現在你知道了，人生不會總是稱心如意的。
Jamie 傑米	Anyways, it's all water under the bridge now. 總之，一切都無法挽回了。

160. make one's hair stand on end　使人害怕

💬 令人毛骨悚然：

A: The horror movie was so scary!
　　那恐怖電影真是恐怖極了！

B: Yeah, it made my hair stand on end.
　　是啊！害怕的我連頭髮都站起來了。

💭 嚇得人寒毛直立：

A: You really made Mr. Brown's hair stand on end.
　　你真的使布朗先生害怕到連頭髮都站起來了。

B: I didn't mean any *harm*!
　　我不是有意的。

* harm	[hɑrm]	名	損傷、損害

161. The walls have ears.　隔牆有耳。

💬 噓，說話小心一點：

A: Keep your voice down! The walls have ears.
　　小聲一點！隔牆有耳。

B: Oh, so this is a secret?
　　喔，這是一個祕密啊？

💭 不小心走漏風聲：

A: How did you know about this? I didn't tell anyone but Tom!
　　你怎麼知道的？我只有跟湯姆說啊！

B: The walls have ears!
　　隔牆有耳！

162. blow the *whistle* on someone / something
揭發；制止某人（或事）

💬 惡行被揭露：

A: The witness blew the *whistle* on the *defense*.
　　那個證人揭發了被告的惡行。

B: Finally there is *justice*.
終於司法有正義了。

💬 同樣的意思：

Someone blew the *whistle* on him and he got caught.
有人揭發了他的壞事，他就被抓了。

* whis·tle	[ˈhwɪsl̩]	名	口哨、汽笛
* de·fense	[dɪˈfɛns]	名	防禦
* jus·tice	[ˈdʒʌstɪs]	名	公平、公正

🎧 *Track 335*

163. *Ignorance* is bliss.　無知便是福。

💬 傻人有傻福：

A: He doesn't know that people are talking behind his back.
他不知道大家在他背後說壞話。

B: *Ignorance* is bliss.
無知便是福。

💬 太聰明也未必是好事：

A: I know nothing about the stocks.
我對股票一無所知。

B: *Ignorance* is bliss. You wouldn't want to know.
無知便是福。你不會想知道的。

* ig·no·rance	[ˈɪgnərəns]	名	無知、不學無術

🎧 *Track 336*

164. take the wind out of one's *sails*　使某人頓時洩氣，威風掃地

💬 真是令人掃興：

A: Jenny was really *eager* to go on a picnic tomorrow.
珍妮真的很期待去明天的野餐。

B: Well, the weather forecast took the wind out of her *sails* when they reported that it will rain tomorrow.
但是當氣象局說明天會下雨的時候，頓時洩了她的氣。

💬 **大失所望：**

A: It's too bad that Oliver wasn't elected the class leader.
奧利佛沒被選上班長真的很可惜。

B: Yes, that really took the wind out of his sails.
是啊，那真的讓他很洩氣。

* ea·ger	['igɚ]	形	渴望的
* sail	[sel]	名	帆、航行

🎧 *Track 337*

165. in the seventh *heaven*　在無比幸福快樂中

💬 **沈迷在熱中事物裡：**

A: I am in the seventh *heaven* when I am in a music concert.
當我在音樂會中，我彷彿處在快樂天堂中。

B: You are really a music lover.
你真的是一個音樂愛好者。

💬 **得償所願：**

A: Sarah was in the seventh *heaven* when she found the book that she really wanted.
當莎拉找到她很想要的書，她好開心。

B: That must be a really interesting book.
那應該是一本很有趣的書。

* heav·en	['hɛvən]	名	天堂

🎧 *Track 338*

166. call a *spade* a *spade*　有話直說

💬 **覺得別人不誠實：**

A: I think you don't always tell me the truth.
我覺得你常常都不告訴我實話。

B: Call a spade a *spade*. You think I lie, don't you?
你有話直說吧！你覺得我會說謊，對吧？

💬 **直言不諱未必都對：**

A: I think everyone should call a *spade* a *spade*.
　　我覺得每一個人都應該有話直說。

B: But being *blunt* sometimes hurts people.
　　可是有時候說話太直會傷人。

* spade	[sped]	名	鏟子
* blunt	[blʌnt]	形	率直的

🎧 *Track 339*

167. Old dogs can't learn new *tricks*.
老狗學不會新把戲；老人不容易適應新東西。

💬 **老套了：**

A: Why don't you teach your dog to sit?
　　你何不教你的狗坐下？

B: Old dogs can't learn new *tricks*.
　　老狗學不會新把戲。

💬 **年紀愈大，通常學習愈慢：**

A: I don't think Harry will learn to play the flute well.
　　我想哈利的長笛學不好的。

B: Yeah, he is already 70 years old. Old dogs can't learn new *tricks*.
　　對啊，他已經 70 歲了，老人比較不容易適應新東西。

* trick	[trɪk]	名	詭計；花招

🎧 *Track 340*

168. *bury* one's head in the *sand*　鴕鳥心態

💬 **避之唯恐不及：**

A: Whenever there is a problem, he *buries* his head in the *sand*.
　　每當一有問題，他就採鴕鳥心態。

B: He has low EQ.
　　他 EQ 很低。

一味逃避：

A: When he asked me to give him an answer, I just *buried* my head in the *sand*.
他叫我給他答案的時候，我出現了鴕鳥心態。

B: You shouldn't have done that.
你不應該那麼做的。

| * bur·y | [ˈbɛrɪ] | 動 | 埋 |
| * sand | [sænd] | 名 | 沙子 |

🎧 *Track 341*

169. You only live once. 人生只有這麼一次（人生不能重來）。

把握當下：

A: Do you think I should spend all my savings on this trip?
你覺得我要把所有的積蓄都花在這旅遊上嗎？

B: Why not? You only live once.
何不呢？人生只有這麼一次！

人生一定要試那麼一次

A: Give me a reason to go bungee-jumping.
給我一個去跳高空彈跳的原因。

B: You only live once.
人生只有這麼一次。

🎧 *Track 342*

🗨️ Chat 不 斷 流

| Billie
比莉 | The way she smiles makes my hair stand on end.
她的笑容真令人害怕。 |
| Jean
珍 | She is not just creepy. I heard she's also an evil person.
她不僅長得很可怕，我聽說她還很邪惡。 |

Billie 比莉	Hey, keep it down. The walls have ears. Do you want her to find out that you're saying these things behind her back? 嘿，小聲點，你想讓她發現你在她背後說這些話嗎？
Jean 珍	What's the big deal? I always call a spade a spade. And one day, I will blow the whistle on her! 有什麼關係？我總是有話直說，總有一天，我會揭發她的！
Billie 比莉	Are you out of your mind? 你瘋了嗎？
Jean 珍	Stop burying your head in the sand. Can't you see she's trying to ruin everything? 別再鴕鳥心態了，你看不出來她想要毀掉一切嗎？
Billie 比莉	No, I don't see it at all. 不，我看不出來。
Jean 珍	Ugh, ignorance is such a bliss! 天啊，無知真的就是福！

🎧 *Track 343*

170. **Home is where the *heart* is.**　家總是讓人思念的地方。

💬 家才是避風港：

A: I feel so relaxed to be home after a long trip.
　　在長期旅遊後回到家，總是讓我覺得很放鬆。

B: Yes, home is where the *heart* is.
　　是啊！家裡總是讓人思念的地方。

💬 相同的表達：

A: Why don't you like Paris?
　　你為什麼不喜歡巴黎？

B: Home is where the *heart* is, and I have never thought of Paris as home.
　　家才是讓人思念的地方，而且我從沒把巴黎當做家。

* heart	[hɑrt]	名	心、中心、核心

171. Every cloud has a *silver* lining.
黑暗中總有一線曙光；否極泰來。

💬 **一線生機：**

A: When I was sick, I realized that every cloud has a *silver* lining.
當我生病的時候，我發現黑暗中的一線曙光。

B: Yeah, you really have many good friends.
對啊！你有許多好朋友。

💬 **苦盡甘來：**

A: I never thought that we could make it to the end.
我從沒想過我們可以撐到最後。

B: I told you, every cloud has a *silver* lining.
我跟你說過啦！否極泰來。

* sil·ver	[ˈsɪlvə]	形	銀色的

172. in any *case*　無論如何

💬 **真的可以放心：**

A: You don't need to worry in any *case*.
無論如何，你都不需要擔心。

B: Are you sure?
你確定嗎？

💬 **必需要完成：**

A: We have to get these done in any *case*.
無論如何，我們都需要把這做好。

B: I don't think that we can make it.
我覺得我們做不完了。

💬 **絕對不可以：**

You shouldn't do this in any *case*.
你們無論如何都不該這麼做。

* case	[kes]	名	情形、情況

173. Good things come to those who wait.
有耐心的人總會嘗到好處（好酒沉甕底）。

等待是有代價的：

A: When can I taste the cookies that you make?
我什麼時候才可以吃到你做的餅乾？

B: Be *patient*! Good things come to those who wait.
有耐心一點，好酒沉甕底！

再多點耐性：

A: Could you give me that CD soon?
你能趕快給我那張 CD 嗎？

B: Good things come to those who wait. I will be finished soon.
有耐心的人才會嚐到甜頭，我快聽完了啦！

* pa·tient	[ˈpeʃənt]	形	忍耐的

174. Where there is a *will*, there is a way.　有志者，事竟成。

勝利是屬於最有毅力的人：

A: I don't know if I could get my master this fall.
我不知道今年秋天我可不可以拿到我的碩士學位。

B: Where there is a *will*, there is a way.
有志者，事竟成。

上天不負苦心人：

A: Do you think Mary could make it to Harvard?
你覺得瑪莉上得了哈佛嗎？

B: She has been studying really hard, and where there is a *will*, there is a way.
她一直很努力的讀書，有志者，事竟成！

* will	[wɪl]	名	意志力

Chapter 02 人際社交 Interpersonal Relationships

175. That's the pot calling the *kettle* black. 龜笑鱉沒尾巴。

💬 **五十步笑百步：**

A: You are such a short man!
你長得好矮哦！

B: That's the pot calling the *kettle* black.
你真是龜笑鱉沒尾巴耶！

💬 **相同的情境：**

A: She called me a miser!
她叫我小氣鬼！

B: That's the pot calling the *kettle* black. She is a miser herself.
真是龜笑鱉沒尾巴耶！她自己也是小氣鬼啊！

* ket·tle	[ˈkɛtl]	名	水壺

176. bang/beat one's head against a brick wall
做徒勞無功的事

💬 **白費心機了：**

A: I *determine* to *persuade* him to go to the party with me.
我決心要說服他跟我一起去參加派對。

B: You are banging your head against a brick wall. He is not going to change his mind.
你根本是白費心力，他不會聽你的啦！

💬 **沒有用的：**

Sally is banging her head against a brick wall trying to change his mind.
莎莉要他改變心意，根本是白費心力。

* de·ter·mine	[dɪˈtɜmɪn]	動	決定
* per·suade	[pəˈswed]	動	說服

177. **An apple a day keeps the doctor away.**
每天一蘋果，醫生遠離我。

💬 養生的好習慣：

A: Why do you eat apples everyday?
你為什麼每天都吃蘋果？

B: Haven't you heard? An apple a day keeps the doctor away.
你沒聽說嗎？每天一蘋果，醫生遠離我。

💬 吃蘋果有好處：

Why don't you eat some apples? An apple a day keeps the doctor away.
你何不吃一些蘋果呢？每天一蘋果，醫生遠離我。

178. **Don't count your chickens before they're *hatched*.**
不要太早打如意算盤。

💬 八字都還沒一撇：

A: I am going to buy a new ring when I get my first salary.
當我拿到第一份薪水的時候，我要買一只新的戒指。

B: Don't count your chickens before they're *hatched*. You haven't even started working yet.
別太早打如意算盤，你根本還沒開始上班。

💬 別做白日夢：

A: Should I buy a new car or a new house when I win the lottery?
如果我中了樂透，我是該買一輛新車還是一棟新房子？

B: How are you *positive* that you will win the lottery? Don't count your chickens before they're *hatched*.
你怎麼確定你就會贏得樂透？別太早打如意算盤！

* hatch	[hætʃ]	動	計畫、孵化
* pos·i·tive	[ˈpɑzətɪv]	形	確信的、積極的

Chapter 02 人際社交 Interpersonal Relationships

179. you dare (to) ...　你敢……

💬 **好大的膽子：**

A: How dare you do something like that!
　　你竟敢做這種事！

B: It's none of your business.
　　不關你的事。

💬 **你有沒有膽子嘗試：**

A: Do you dare to jump off that wall?
　　你敢跳下那座牆嗎？

B: I dare not.
　　我不敢。

💬 **表達同樣的意思：**

You dare to ask her in person?
你敢親自問她嗎？

* dare	[dɛr]	動	敢、挑戰

180. **I don't believe so.**　我不這麼認為。

💬 **持不同意見：**

A: I think she is very *honest*.
　　我覺得她很誠實。

B: I don't believe so.
　　我不這麼認為。

💬 **不以為然：**

A: I did my best on the test.
　　這次考試我已經盡我的全力了。

B: I don't believe so.
　　我不這麼認為。

* hon·est	['ɑnɪst]	形	誠實的、耿直的

181. How could you stand...?　你怎麼受得了……？

💬 **忍耐力很強：**

A: It's very hot in Taiwan.
台灣的天氣很熱。

B: How could you stand staying here all summer?
你怎麼受得了待在台灣一整個夏天？

💬 **相同意思的表達：**

A: My brother is very *noisy*.
我弟弟很吵。

B: How could you stand him then?
你怎麼受得了他？

* nois·y	[ˈnɔɪzɪ]	形	嘈雜的、喧鬧的

182. live and *learn*　活到老學到老

💬 **大開眼界：**

A: I didn't know that you can watch TV on computer.
我不知道在電腦上也可以看電視！

B: Well, live and *learn*.
活一天長一天見聞囉。

💬 **真是前所未聞：**

A: I didn't know Kerry is a dentist.
我不知道凱瑞是一個牙醫。

B: Live and *learn*.
活一天長一天見聞囉。

* learn	[lɝn]	動	學習

183. It's not the end of the world. 不是世界末日。

💬 下一個會更好：

A: I don't know what to do without Joey.
我不知道我沒了喬伊我該怎麼辦？

B: It's not the end of the world. You will be fine.
又不是世界末日，你會很好的！

💬 再找就會有了：

A: I lost my job. What am I going to do?
我沒工作了，我該怎麼辦？

B: It's not the end of the world. You will find a new job very soon.
又不是世界末日，你很快就會找到新工作的！

184. cost someone a pretty penny 很貴

💬 用了畢生積蓄：

A: Wow! That ring must have cost you a pretty penny!
哇！那戒指一定花了你很多錢！

B: Yes, I spent all my savings on it.
是的，我把我所有的積蓄都花在那上面了！

💬 要價不斐：

That car cost me a pretty penny.
那輛車花了我很多錢！

🐱Chat 不斷流

Frankie 法蘭琪	Can't believe I got fired. 不敢相信我被開除了。
Lola 蘿拉	It's not the end of the world. Every cloud has a silver lining. You will get offered a better position eventually. 又不是世界末日，事情總會否極泰來，你會找到更好的工作。
Frankie 法蘭琪	I dare not believe so. I feel like I'm just banging my head against a brick wall. 我不敢想，我覺得自己好像在做徒勞無功的事
Lola 蘿拉	Don't say that. Where there is a will, there is a way. 別這麼說，有志者，事竟成。
Frankie 法蘭琪	Guess I will have to keep trying in any case. 也許無論如何，我都該不斷嘗試。
Lola 蘿拉	That's the spirit. Good things come to those who wait! 這樣想就對了，有耐心的人總會得到好處！

Chapter 3

職場應對

Business Conversation

Chapter 03 音檔雲端連結

因各家手機系統不同,若無法直接掃描,
仍可以至以下電腦雲端連結下載收聽。
(https://tinyurl.com/p2xz4sbt)

🗨 Chat 聊不停

🎧 *Track 359*

01. **Hold on.** 請稍等。

💬 **可以留言嗎：**

A: May I leave a message, please?
我能留言嗎？

B: Hold on.
請稍等。

💬 **立即轉接：**

A: Hello, may I speak to Mary, please?
哈囉！我可不可以跟瑪麗說話？

B: Hold on.
請等一下。

💬 **請等我一下：**

Hold on. I'll come back to you soon.
請稍等，我稍後回來。

🎧 *Track 360*

02. **God! What the hell are you doing?** 天呀！你到底在幹嘛？

💬 **只是畫畫而已：**

A: God! What the hell are you doing?
天呀！你到底在幹嘛？

B: Drawing.
畫畫。

💬 **覺得莫名奇妙：**

A: God! What the hell are you doing?
天呀！你到底在幹嘛？

B: Cleaning your room.
清理你的房間。

Chapter 03 職場應對 *Business Conversation*

03. **Come on. Just go along with it.** 好啦！將就一點嘛。

💬 就勉為其難吧：

A: This is a dirty place.
這裡真髒。

B: Come on. Just go along with it.
好啦！將就一點嘛。

💬 也可以這樣用：

A: This place is small.
這裡真小。

B: Come on. Just go along with it.
好啦！將就一點嘛！

04. **I just don't understand...** 我就是想不通……

💬 找不到原因：

A: He's acting *weird*.
他表現得怪怪的。

B: I just don't understand why.
我就是想不通為什麼。

💬 無法理解他人：

A: He likes to be alone.
他喜歡自己一個人。

B: I just don't understand why.
我就是想不通為什麼。

💬 為什麼不知道呢：

I just don't understand why she doesn't know the answer.
我就是想不通為什麼她不知道答案。

| * weird | [wɪrd] | 形 | 怪異的、不可思議的 |

05. **So far, so good.**　目前為止一切都好。

💬 應該很不錯：

A: So how is your new job?
你的新工作如何啊？

B: So far, so good. My boss is really nice.
到現在一切都好，我老闆人很親切。

💬 感覺很好：

A: How are you getting along with your boyfriend?
你和你男朋友相處得如何？

B: So far, so good.
到現在一切都很好！

06. **Good for you!**　好啊！做得好！

💬 太好的決定了：

A: Lucy and I are getting married.
我和露西要結婚ㄌ！

B: Good for you! Congratulations!
好啊！恭喜囉！

💬 表現很棒啊：

A: My boss loved my *proposal* and decided to give me a raise.
老闆很喜歡我的提案，並決定給我加薪呢！

B: Good for you!
做得好！

* pro·pos·al	[prə`pozəl]	名	提議

07. The rest is history. 眾所皆知。

💬 結果有目共睹：

A: The company started with only two people, and the rest is history.
這公司一開始時只有兩個人，其他的大家都知道了。

B: It's amazing that it has *branches* all over the world now, isn't it?
公司現在在全世界都有分公司，真的很神奇吧？

🗨 毋需贅言：

A: Why did you go to the States?
你幹嘛去美國？

B: I wanted to study and the rest is history.
我本來想要讀書，剩下的大家都知道了！

* branch	[bræntʃ]	名	分店、分公司

08. A little bird told me. 我聽說的

💬 壞事傳千里：

A: How did you know that our company is having *financial* problems?
你怎麼知道我們公司有財務上的困難？

B: A little bird told me.
我聽説的。

🗨 流言傳來傳去：

A: How did you know how much he makes a month?
你怎麼知道他一個月賺多少？

B: A little bird told me.
我聽説的。

* fi·nan·cial	[faɪˋnænʃəl]	形	金融的、財政的

09. **Mind your own business.** 別多管閒事;不關你的事

💬 **不想回答:**

A: How much do you make a month?
你一個月賺多少錢?

B: Can you mind your own business? That's a very *personal* question.
不關你的事,那是一個很私人的問題。

💬 **我喜歡就好:**

A: Why don't you *paint* it white instead?
你為什麼不改塗白色的?

B: Can you mind your own business? I like red.
你別多管閒事,我喜歡紅色的。

| * per·son·al | [ˈpɜsnl] | 形 | 個人的 |
| * paint | [pent] | 動 | 粉刷、繪畫 |

10. **That's news to me.** 這可是新聞呢。

💬 **前所未聞:**

A: Did you hear that the old department store is going to be closed down?
你有沒有聽說那家老的百貨公司要關門了。

B: No. That's news to me!
沒有,還頭一次聽說呢。

💬 **第一次聽到消息:**

A: I heard that you got promoted to manager.
我聽說你被升為經理了啊!

B: Really? That's news to me.
真的嗎?這對我來說還真是新聞呢!

Chapter 03 職場應對 Business Conversation

🐾 Chat 不斷流

James 詹姆士	Hey, I heard you want to ask Rosie out. 嘿，聽說你想約蘿西出去。
Michael 麥可	Hold on, how do you know? 等等，你怎麼知道？
James 詹姆士	A little bird told me. Good for you, man. She is both the prettiest and the smartest girl I know. 我聽說的。很好啊，老兄，她是我認識的女生中，最漂亮也最聰明的。
Michael 麥可	I just don't understand why she dated that idiot, Jack. 我就是想不通她之前為什麼跟傑克那個呆瓜在一起。
James 詹姆士	He took her to see her favorite band, and the rest is history. 傑克帶她去看她最愛的樂團，其他事情大家都知道了。
Michael 麥可	That's news to me. 這對我來說可是新聞呢。
James 詹姆士	Here, give me your phone. I'm sending her a text for you. 手機拿來，我幫你傳簡訊給她。
Michael 麥可	God, what the hell are you doing? Don't do it! 天呀！你在搞什麼？不要傳！
James 詹姆士	Come on. Just go along with it. I'm sure she wants to go out with you, too. 好啦！就這樣做嘛，我相信她也想跟你出去。
Michael 麥可	Mind your own business! 別多管閒事。
James 詹姆士	I was just trying to help! 我只是想幫忙而已！

11. **You've got me there.** 你考倒我了。

💬 我不知道：

A: What does the word "loony" mean?
"loony" 這個字是什麼意思？

B: You've got me there.
你考倒我了。

💬 問問別人吧：

A: Will the president arrive at noon?
總裁中午會到這裡嗎？

B: You've got me there. Why don't you ask Harry?
你考倒我了，你問哈利好了。

12. **Can you *handle* it?** 做得來吧？

💬 輕而易舉：

A: Can you *handle* it?
你可以做得來嗎？

B: No problem!
沒問題。

💬 事情有難度：

A: It's a pretty hard job. Can you *handle* it?
這工作很難，你做得來嗎？

B: I will try my best.
我會盡力的。

* han·dle	[ˈhændl]	動	處理、對付

Chapter 03 職場應對 *Business Conversation*

13. burn the *candle* at both ends
白天忙碌，晚上也要忙；花費很多精力（蠟燭兩頭燒）

💬 **創業維艱：**

A: Your new business seems to be going very well.
你的新生意看起來經營得不錯喔！

B: Well, I had to burn the *candle* at both ends in the beginning.
剛開始的時候我得花費很多精力！

💬 **不分晝夜的努力苦讀：**

I was burning the *candle* at both ends to pass this exam.
我得從早到晚辛勤的讀書才能通過這考試。

* can·dle	[ˋkændl̩]	名	蠟燭、燭光

14. meet a / the *deadline* 截稿

💬 **期限快到了：**

A: Do you want to go to the movies with us?
你要不要跟我們一起去看電影？

B: No, I have to meet the *deadline* on my mid-term report.
不行，我的期中報告得快點交了。

💬 **固定的截止日期：**

We have a *deadline* to meet every week at the magazine company.
我們在雜誌社，每一個星期都要截稿。

* dead·line	[ˋdɛdˏlaɪn]	名	限期

15. step on someone's toes   觸怒到某人

💬 **踩到別人的地雷：**

A: Why don't you ask her how much she makes a month?
你何不問問她一個月賺多少錢？

B: I don't want to step on her toes by asking such a personal question.
我才不要因問她這麼一個私人的問題而激怒她呢。

💬 **四面楚歌：**

I am getting a *transfer* because I have stepped on too many people's toes since I came to this office.
我在辦理調職，因為自從來到這辦公室，我已經激怒了許多人。

* trans·fer	[træns`fɝ]	名	遷移、調職

16. Give *credit* where *credit* is *due*.   稱讚該被讚美的人。

💬 **謙讓不居功：**

A: You did a great job on this report.
你這個報告做得很好！

B: Give *credit* where *credit* it *due*. Joe was the one who put it all together.
你該稱讚該被稱讚的人，喬是把它全部組合起來的人。

💬 **誇錯對象了：**

A: Hey! That painting of yours is great!
你的那幅畫真棒！

B: Give *credit* where *credit* is *due*. I didn't paint the picture, Mary did.
你該稱讚該被稱讚的人，這畫不是我畫的，是瑪麗畫的。

* cred·it	[`krɛdɪt]	名	功勞、讚揚
* due	[dju]	形	合適的

17. step over the line　太過分了

🗨 加倍奉還：

A: You better say sorry to her. You step over the line this time.
你最好跟她説對不起，這次你太過分了。

B: She hit me first.
她先打我的。

💭 超越分際，以下犯上：

A: Why is the boss so angry this morning?
今天早上老闆怎麼那麼生氣？

B: It's because what Larry said at the meeting step over the line.
因為賴瑞在會議上説的話太過分了。

🗨 讓人看不過去：

The girl's rude *behaviors* surely step over the line.
那女孩的魯莽行為實在太過分了。

* be·hav·ior	[bɪˋhevjɚ]	名	舉止、行為

18. go from bad to worse　每況愈下

🗨 愈來愈走下坡：

A: How is your business?
你的生意如何？

B: It is going from bad to worse. I think I will have to close down the shop very soon.
它每況愈下！我想我很快就會把店關起來了。

🗨 病情日漸惡化：

A: How is your mother? Is she *recovering* from the cold?
你媽媽好嗎？她的感冒復原了嗎？

B: No, her cold has gone from bad to worse.
還沒，她的感冒越來越嚴重了。

* re·cov·er	[rɪˋkʌvɚ]	動	恢復、重新獲得

19. **No pains, no gains.** 一分耕耘，一分收穫。

💬 **要先付出才可能有收穫：**

A: I have been working so hard that I have been *neglecting* my family.
我一直努力工作，都忽略了我的家庭。

B: No pains, no gains. You are making really good money now. But family is also important.
一分耕耘，一分收穫。你現在賺很多錢，但家庭也是很重要的。

💬 **犧牲是有代價的：**

A: I have finally finished writing this book, but I have missed all the good movies this month.
我終於寫完這本書了，但是我也錯過了這個月所有的好電影。

B: No pains, no gains. This is going to be a great book.
一分耕耘，一分收穫。這將是一本很棒的書。

* ne·glect	[nɪˋglɛkt]	動	疏忽

20. **Don't rock the boat!** 不要破壞現狀、搗亂。

💬 **沒事找事，惹事生非：**

A: Should we go on a strike?
我們要不要罷工遊行？

B: Don't rock the boat when everything is going so well.
現在一切都這麼好，不要破壞現狀！

💬 **不要節外生枝：**

Don't rock the boat! You are not going to win the presidential election by blackening your opponents' names.
不要打亂計畫。你不會藉由抹黑對手而贏得總統大選。

Chapter 03 職場應對 Business Conversation

 Chat 不斷流

Peter 彼得	Helen, I'm working late tonight. 海倫，我今晚要加班。
Helen 海倫	Again? 又要加班？
Peter 彼得	Can you handle it? 妳能應付嗎？
Helen 海倫	Don't step over the line! I can't look after the kids on my own! 別太過分了！我沒辦法一個人照顧孩子！
Peter 彼得	Please, just one more night. 拜託，就再這麼一個晚上。
Helen 海倫	I'm trying to meet a deadline at work. I've been burning the candle at both ends! 我要趕截稿，我最近都蠟燭兩頭燒！
Peter 彼得	I know you're busy, but there's nothing I can do. 我知道妳很忙，但我真的沒辦法幫忙。
Helen 海倫	My health condition has also gone from bad to worse. 我的健康狀況也每況愈下。
Peter 彼得	I'm really sorry. My boss wants me to stay later tonight. I promise I will come home as soon as possible. 真的很抱歉，老闆要我今晚在公司待晚一點，我答應會盡快趕回來。
Helen 海倫	Fine. 好吧。

21. worth its weight in *gold*　很有價值的

💭 好好存放，比較保險：

A: That file is worth its weight in *gold*.
那資料很有價值。

B: Then we better keep it in some safe place.
那我們最好把它放在一個安全的地方。

💬 賺錢金童：

A: He has *earned* a lot of money for his company.
他為他的公司賺了很多錢。

B: Then he's worth his weight in *gold*.
那麼他是很有價值的喔！

* earn	[ɚn]	動	賺取、得到
* gold	[gold]	名	金子

22. Great minds think alike.　英雄所見略同。

💭 雙方持相同見解：

A: It's so surprising that Wal-Mart and 7-Eleven make the same decision to develope their chains in China.
Wal-Mart 和 7-11 竟然都決定要到中國發展。

B: Great minds think alike. People are very *optimistic* of business opportunities in China.
英雄所見略同，大家都看好中國商機囉。

💬 大多數人的看法一致：

As the saying goes, "great minds think alike," so many CEOs would make the similar decision when they are faced with problems.
俗話說「英雄所見略同」，所以許多公司的總裁在面臨問題時會有類似的決定。

* op·ti·mis·tic	[ˌɑptəˈmɪstɪk]	形	樂觀（主義）的

Chapter 03 職場應對 Business Conversation

23. **I wish to talk to you alone.** 我想和你私下談談。

💬 想知道些什麼：

A: I wish to talk to you alone.
我想和你私下談談。

B: About what?
有關於什麼？

💬 不能公開說的對話：

A: Do you want to talk to me?
你想跟我談談嗎？

B: Yes, I wish to talk to you alone.
是的，我想和你私下談談。

24. **It's not likely.** 可能不是這樣。

💬 不認同別人的想法：

A: She is a strange person.
她是一個很奇怪的人。

B: It's not likely.
可能不是這樣。

💬 有隱情：

A: Is he mad?
他瘋了嗎？

B: It's not likely.
可能不是這樣。

💬 不敢肯定，只是猜測：

It's not likely that she knows you from before.
她之前可能不認識你。

25. You learn something new every day.
你每天都會學到新東西／知道新事情。

💬 **頭條新聞：**

A: Mary has been promoted as the president of her company.
瑪莉被升為她公司的經理。

B: I learn something new every day.
這可是我頭一次聽到。

💬 **無奇不有：**

A: I didn't know you can fix cars by yourself.
我不知道你會自己修車。

B: Well, you learn something new every day.
真是每天都有新鮮事哪！

26. *wrap* things up　把事情整理一番，做個結束。

💬 **設定進度：**

A: Are you leaving yet?
你要走了沒？

B: I want to *wrap* things up here before I go home.
我在回家前想要把東西告一段落。

💬 **收尾：**

Before I go home, I will have to *wrap* things up.
在我回家前，我得把事情做個結束。

* wrap	[ræp]	動	包裝

Chapter 03 職場應對 Business Conversation

27. Never put off *until* tomorrow what you can do today.
今日事，今日畢。

💬 不要再拖了：

A: Can I do this tomorrow?
我可以明天再做這個嗎？

B: Never put off *until* tomorrow what you can do today.
今日事，今日畢。

💬 按進度完成：

A: Let's finish this before we go home.
我們回家前將這個做好。

B: Yup, never put off *until* tomorrow what you can do today.
是啊，今天可以做的事就今天做吧！

| * un·til/till | [ənˋtɪl]/[tɪl] | 連 | 直到……為止 |

28. pretend...　假裝……

💬 別裝了：

A: Let's pretend it's mine.
讓我們假裝這是我的。

B: Don't be *childish*.
別那麼幼稚。

💬 故意假裝：

A: Pretend that you like it.
假裝你喜歡這個。

B: Why?
為什麼？

💬 虛情假意好難：

Pretending to like someone who you dislike is frustrating.
假裝自己去喜歡一個討厭的人很煩。

| * child·ish | [ˋtʃaɪldɪʃ] | 形 | 孩子氣的 |

29. It's better not to talk about it.　還是別說好了。

💬 嘘，小心隔牆有耳：

A: I don't like my boss.
　 我不喜歡我的老闆。

B: It's better not to talk about it.
　 還是別說好了。

💭 心知肚明就好：

A: I don't like the food.
　 我不喜歡這些食物。

B: It's better not to talk about it.
　 還是別說好了。

🗨 Chat 不 斷 流

Miranda 米蘭達	Hey Bethany, I wish to talk to you alone. 貝思妮，我想和妳私下談談。
Bethany 貝思妮	Sure, what's up? 當然，怎麼了？
Miranda 米蘭達	Do you think Sally is pretending to be my friend? 妳覺得莎莉是不是假裝當我朋友？
Bethany 貝思妮	It's not likely. Why do you think that? 可能不是這樣吧，妳怎麼會這樣想？
Miranda 米蘭達	Well, some things are better left unsaid. 有些事最好還是不要說。
Bethany 貝思妮	If you don't let me know the reason. I won't know how to help you. 如果妳不告訴我原因，我就無法幫助妳。

Miranda 米蘭達	I just feel like she is always trying to bring me down. 我只是覺得她常常打擊我。
Bethany 貝思妮	Nah, I'm pretty sure it's nothing personal. That's just how she is. She thinks she is worth her weight in gold. 不，我蠻確定她不是針對妳，這只是她的本性，她覺得自己價值連城。
Miranda 米蘭達	Really? I didn't know that about her. 真的？我還真不知道她是這樣的人。
Bethany 貝思妮	You learn something new every day. 妳每天都會學到新東西。
Miranda 米蘭達	Alright, let's wrap things up and go home. 好吧，我們把事情結束，回家吧。
Bethany 貝思妮	Let's do it! 來吧！

🎧 *Track 391*

30. I wouldn't know! 你問我，我問誰？

💬 **自己不會看哦：**

A: What's the date today?
今天幾號？

B: I wouldn't know!
你問我，我問誰？

💬 **沒有人知道：**

A: What's her name?
她叫什麼名字？

B: I wouldn't know!
你問我，我問誰？

31. come out in the wash 真相大白；得到圓滿的結果

💬 努力會有收穫的：

A: We have worked so hard on this *project*.
我們為了這計畫很努力。

B: It will all come out in the wash.
總是會有好的成果的。

💬 事情會圓滿落幕的：

A: There are a lot of things to do.
還有好多事要做喔！

B: Don't worry. All things will come out in the wash.
別擔心！所有的事都會圓滿達成的。

* proj·ect	[ˈprɑdʒɛkt]	名	計畫

32. **What number did you call?** 你打幾號？

💬 打錯電話了：

A: The number that you gave me is wrong.
你給我的電話號碼是錯的。

B: What number did you call?
你打幾號？

💬 沒有這個人：

A: May I speak to Julian, please?
請問朱力恩在嗎？

B: What number did you call? There is no Julian here.
你打幾號啊？這裡沒有朱力恩。

33. **Give ...a call.** 打電話給……

💬 報平安:

A: Give me a call when you get home.
你到家打給我。

B: OK.
好。

💬 取消約會:

A: I am not feeling well. I think I will stay home tonight.
我不舒服,我想我今晚就待在家吧!

B: Give Jenny a call. She is *expecting* you.
那你打給珍妮吧!她在等你呢。

💬 有事情要在電話裡談:

Give Daisy a call when you are free.
等你有空的時候打個電話給黛西。

* ex·pect	[ɪkˋspɛkt]	動	期望

34. **Could I speak to...** 請找……

💬 打電話找人:

A: Hello, could I speak to Gary?
喂?請問蓋瑞在不在?

B: Hold on a second.
請等一下。

💬 可以幫我轉接電話嗎:

A: Hello, could I speak to Dr. Lin?
哈囉!我可不可以跟林醫師說話?

B: I'm *afraid* you have the wrong number.
我想你打錯電話了。

* a·fraid	[əˋfred]	形	害怕的、擔心的

35. You have the wrong number.　你打錯了。

💬 **沒有這個人：**

A: Is Frankie there?
　法蘭琪在嗎？

B: You have the wrong number.
　你打錯電話了。

💬 **抱歉，打錯電話了：**

A: You have the wrong number.
　你打錯電話了。

B: I am sorry.
　對不起。

36. Who was it? / Who called?　誰打來的電話？

💬 **詢問是誰來電：**

A: Who was it?
　誰打來了？

B: Wrong number.
　打錯的。

💬 **也可以這樣問：**

A: Who called?
　誰打來的電話？

B: It was Jeff. He was asking if he could come over tonight.
　是傑夫，他問他今天晚上可不可以過來。

37. This is ... speaking.　我是……。

💬 你是誰：

A: Who is speaking?
誰啊？

B: This is Sharon speaking.
我是莎朗。

💬 自己報上大名：

A: This is Tom speaking. May I help you?
我是湯姆。我可以幫你嗎？

B: Yes, I want to make a reservation.
是的，我想要訂位。

38. I'll call you back later.　待會回電給你。

💬 晚一點再繼續聊：

A: I need to take the trash out now. I'll call you back later.
我現在要把垃圾拿出去，我等一下再打給你。

B: Sure.
沒問題。

💬 熱線電話先暫停：

A: My parents are home. I'll call you back later.
我爸媽回來了。待會打給你。

B: OK. Bye.
好，拜拜。

💬 先忙其他的事：

I am busy and I'll call you back later.
我現在很忙，待會回電給你。

39. Don't speak too soon.   話別說太早。

💬 **別言之過早了：**

A: This is the lowest price on the *market*.
這是市場上最低的價格了。

B: Don't speak too soon. The Brown Company has already offered a lower price.
話別說得太早，布朗公司已經給了一個更低的價格了。

💬 **別掉以輕心：**

A: I am sure I am going to pass this exam.
我很確定我會通過這一次的考試。

B: Don't speak too soon. I heard the test is really hard this time.
話別說得太早，我聽說這次的考試真的很難。

* mar·ket	[ˈmɑrkɪt]	名	市場

 Chat 不 斷 流

Wendy 溫蒂	Hello? 喂？
Vincent 文森	Could I speak to Lori, please? 請找羅芮。
Wendy 溫蒂	There's no Lori here. 這裡沒有羅芮。
Vincent 文森	What? 什麼？
Wendy 溫蒂	I think you have the wrong number. 我想你打錯了。

Chapter 03 職場應對 *Business Conversation*

Vincent 文森	Oh, sorry about that. 噢，很抱歉。
Wendy 溫蒂	Bye! 再見！
Eric 艾端克	Who was that? 誰打來的電話？
Wendy 溫蒂	I wouldn't know! Wrong number. He was trying to give "Lori" a call. There is no Lori here! 你問我，我問誰？他打錯電話，說要找「羅芮」，我們這裡沒有羅芮！

🎧 *Track 402*

40. **There is no such thing as a free lunch.**
天下沒有白吃的午餐。

💬 吃人嘴軟拿人手短：

A: Could you give me your blue shirt? I really like it.
你可不可以給我你藍色的上衣？我真的好喜歡。

B: Then you will have to help me with the laundry. There is no such thing as a free lunch.
那你得幫我洗衣服，天下沒有白吃的午餐。

💬 沒有不勞而獲的事：

A: My company is offering me a free trip to Hawaii.
我公司要讓我免費去一趟夏威夷！

B: You better check it out. There is no such thing as a free lunch.
你最好問清楚，天下沒有白吃的午餐。

41. know the *ropes*   知道、學習規則或內容

💬 **新手上路，請多多指教：**

A: I am new to the office, so I don't know the *ropes* yet.
我剛來這辦公室，很多事我還不懂。

B: That's OK. I will show you around.
沒問題。我會帶你到處看看的。

💬 **失去了才懂得珍惜：**

A: We really miss Sarah.
我們很想念莎拉。

B: Yeah, she is the only one that knows the *ropes* around here.
是啊，她是唯一知道這裡東西的人。

* rope	[rop]	名	規則、繩

42. Look before you *leap*.   三思而後行。

💬 **想清楚再行動：**

A: I want to quit my job. 我想要辭職。

B: It is not easy to find a job nowadays. You better look before you *leap*.
現在找工作很不容易，你最好要三思而後行。

💬 **投資有風險要小心：**

A: Harry is going to spend all his savings on the *stocks*.
哈利要將他所有的錢花在股票上。

B: He should really look before he *leaps*.
他真的應該三思而後行。

* leap	[lip]	動	使跳過
* stock	[stɑk]	名	股票

Chapter 03 職場應對 Business Conversation

43. bet one's bottom dollar　確信無疑

💬 **自信滿滿：**

A: I bet my bottom dollar on getting that job.
我很確定我一定會得到那份工作。

B: You are really *confident*!
你真的很有信心！

💬 **有夢最美：**

A: I bet my bottom dollar on winning the lottery.
我很確信我會贏得彩券。

B: Well, if you were that sure.
哦，如果你那麼確定的話。

* con·fi·dent	[ˈkɑnfədənt]	形	有信心的

44. take the good with the bad　好的與壞的都要一起接受

💬 **魚與熊掌難以兼得：**

A: My transfer to Paris seems to be interesting and the pay is pretty good, but then I will really miss my parents.
我調到巴黎工作似乎將會很有趣，而且薪水又很好，但是我將會很想我的父母。

B: You have to take the good with the bad.
你好的與壞的都要一起接受。

💬 **有一好沒兩好：**

I make a lot of money by writing, but I guess I have to take the good with the bad: my back hurts a lot because of sitting too long.
我寫文章賺很多錢，但是我好的與壞的都要一起接受：我的腰因為坐太久而痠痛。

45. go back to *square* one　回到原點

💬 **做白工：**

A: We are going back to *square* one on this plan.
　我們在這個計畫上要回到原點了。

B: It's too bad. We don't have enough money.
　很遺憾，我們沒有足夠的錢。

💭 **白忙一場：**

A: The boss did not like our proposal.
　老闆並不喜歡我們的提案。

B: It looks like we better go back to *square* one and think of something else.
　看來我們只好回到原點，然後想一些特別的吧。

* square	[skwɛr]	名	正方形、廣場

46. Leave well enough alone.
維持現狀；對現在已經很滿意了，不用變更。

💬 **不需要幫忙：**

A: Should we help David finish painting the walls?
　我們要不要幫大衛把牆壁粉刷完？

B: Leave well enough alone. He is doing a good job.
　不用了，他自己就做得很好了。

💭 **做得夠好了：**

A: Did you change anything in my play?
　你有在我的劇本裡改變什麼？

B: No, it looks very interesting, so I decided to leave well enough alone.
　不用了，它已經很有趣了，所以我決定就讓它維持現狀。

47. breathe down someone's neck　緊跟在某人後面；監督某人

💬 緊迫盯人：

A: I can't stand Anne anymore. She is always breathing down my neck.
我再也不能忍受安妮了，她總是監督著我。

B: Well, she is your *supervisor*.
她是你的上司啊！

💬 你是跟屁蟲嗎：

Get away from me! You are practically breathing down my neck!
離我遠一點！你不要老是緊跟著我！

* su·per·vi·sor	[ˌsupɚˈvaɪzɚ]	名	監督者、管理人

48. fill someone's shoes　接替某人的職位

💬 誰會來接任：

A: Do you know who is going to fill Peter's shoes?
你知道誰要去接替彼特的職位嗎？

B: I don't know.
我不知道。

💬 擔心能不能勝任新職務：

A: I don't know if I could fill Mary's shoes well.
我不知道我可不可以勝任瑪麗的職位。

B: Don't worry! You will be fine!
別擔心！你會做得很好的！

49. I could hardly catch my breath.　我快忙不過來了。

💬 忙得不可開交：

A: How is everything going?
你忙的如何了？

B: I got tons of work to do. I could hardly catch my breath.
我還有好多事要做，我快忙不過來了。

A: There are so many people in the shop. I could hardly catch my breath.
店裡有好多人，我快忙不過來了。

B: Need some help?
你需要幫忙嗎？

🎮 Chat 不 斷 流

Janet 珍娜	These managers are always breathing down my neck. 這些經理老跟在我後面，監視我。
Angela 安琪拉	There is no such thing as a free lunch. You get paid this much for a good reason. 天下沒有白吃的午餐，你薪水這麼高是有原因的。
Janet 珍娜	I could hardly catch my breath. I need to quit! 我快忙不過來了，我要辭職！
Angela 安琪拉	Better look before you leap. I bet my bottom dollar that you will regret it! 你最好三思而後行，我保證你一定會後悔！
Janet 珍娜	Maybe I won't! 或許我不會後悔！
Angela 安琪拉	You'd have to go back to square one, but they will find someone to fill your shoes very soon. 你必須回到原點，但他們不用多久就會找到人接替你的職位了。
Janet 珍娜	I've made up my mind. 我心意已決。
Angela 安琪拉	Suit yourself. 隨便你。

50. end of the road   終點;最後

💬 仍舉棋不定:

A: Have you *reached* the end of the road by making the final decision yet?
你們做出最後的決定了沒?

B: Not yet.
還沒。

💬 放大假,慰勞自己:

I have been working on this project very hard for a long time. I am planning a nice vacation at the end of the road.
我為這計畫辛勤工作好一陣子了,我要在做完它的時候好好放一個假。

* reach	[ritʃ]	動	到達、伸手拿東西

51. just what the doctor ordered   正合需要

💬 心有靈犀一點通:

A: Do you want to go for a swim?
你要不要去游泳啊?

B: That's just what the doctor ordered.
正合我需要呢!

💬 正中下懷:

A: The boss decided to give us a *raise*.
老闆決定給我們加薪!

B: A raise is just what the doctor ordered.
加薪正合我的需要呢!

* raise	[rez]	名	加薪

52. **Let's call it a day.**　今天到此為止吧！

💬 該結束了：

A: Let's call it a day! I am so tired.
今天到此為止吧！我好累喔！

B: Alright.
好！

💬 同樣的意思：

A: Let's call it a day. We will work on it tomorrow.
今天到此為止吧！我們明天再繼續。

B: Good idea! I am exhausted.
好主意！我累翻了。

53. **You're so difficult!**　你很龜毛耶！

💬 三心二意，搖擺不定：

A: I don't know which one to buy.
我不知道要買哪一個？

B: Samuel, you are so difficult!
山繆，你真龜毛！

💬 挑剔之人：

A: Sharon is such a difficult person.
莎朗真是很龜毛。

B: Everybody knows that.
每一個人都知道。

Chapter 03 職場應對 *Business Conversation*

54. If...　如果……

💬 **我也不知道：**

　A: If you know the answer, please tell me.
　　　如果你知道答案，請告訴我。

　B: I am afraid I don't know.
　　　恐怕我不知道。

💬 **千金難買早知道：**

　A: If I had listened to my mother, things wouldn't have been like this.
　　　如果我當時聽了我媽媽的話，事情就不會這樣了。

　B: Can you stop complaining?
　　　你可以停止抱怨嗎？

💬 **換位思考：**

　If I were you, I would tell him the truth.
　如果我是你，我會說他說實話。

55. Frankly speaking,...　坦白說

💬 **從實招來：**

　A: Frankly speaking, I don't like Joe.
　　　坦白說，我不喜歡喬。

　B: Neither do I.
　　　我也不喜歡。

💬 **說實在的：**

　A: Frankly speaking, I think the party was a *failure*.
　　　坦白說，我覺得派對很失敗。

　B: You are right.
　　　你說的沒錯。

💬 **真心不騙：**

　Frankly speaking, I don't know the answer.
　坦白說，我不知道答案。

* fail·ure	[ˈfeljə]	名	失敗、失策

56. It means ...　這表示……

💬 幫我說明一下：

A: What does this sign say?
　　這標示上寫什麼？

B: It means no dogs are allowed in the park.
　　它的意思是説狗不可以帶進公園。

💬 這什麼意思：

A: What does the word "delusion" mean?
　　"delusion" 這個字是什意思？

B: It means false *belief*.
　　它的意思是妄想。

💬 顯而易見：

It means she likes you.
這表示她喜歡你。

* be·lief	[br'lif]	名	相信、信念

57. Could you *repeat* that?　請再重複一次好嗎？

💬 請再說一次：

A: Could you *repeat* that? I didn't get it.
　　你可不可以再説一次？我沒聽懂。

B: Sure! I will say it again.
　　沒問題，我會再説一次。

💬 有沒有在聽：

A: Could you *repeat* that?
　　你可不可以重複一遍？

B: No! I have said it three times already.
　　不要！我已經説了三次了！

* re·peat	[rɪ'pit]	動	重複

58. It didn't *occur* to me... 我沒想到……

💭 覺得沒可能發生的事：

A: It didn't *occur* to me that I would see you here.
我沒想到我會在這裡見到你。

B: Neither did I.
我也沒想到。

💭 出人意表：

A: It didn't *occur* to me that you would get lost.
我沒想到你會迷路。

B: I'm sorry for being late.
很抱歉我遲到了。

💭 事情超乎預期：

It didn't *occur* to me that things would be like this.
我沒想到事情會變成這樣。

* oc·cur	[əˋkɝ]	動	發生

59. Let me think... 讓我想想……

💭 我再考慮一下：

A: Two thousand dollars is my best offer.
兩千元是我最後的底限。

B: Let me think about it.
讓我想一想。

💭 出主意：

A: I am so bored.
我好無聊喔。

B: Let me think of what to do.
讓我想一下要做什麼。

Let me think of what you may need.
讓我想想你可能需要什麼。

🎧 *Track 423*

📱 Chat 不斷流

Joel 喬爾	Let's call it a day. I'm tired. 今天到此為止吧！我累了。
Sasha 莎夏	No, we're not done yet! 不，我們還沒好。
Joel 喬爾	Let's just wrap it up! 我們趕快收尾吧！
Sasha 莎夏	If we could just work on it for ten more minutes, I think the result is going to come out much nicer. 如果我們能多努力十分鐘，成果會好很多的。
Joel 喬爾	No way! It's good enough! 不用了，已經夠好了！
Sasha 莎夏	Let me think. How about we do another scene of her jumping off the bridge? 我想想，我們再拍一幕，讓她從橋上跳下去如何？
Joel 喬爾	Could you repeat that? 請再重複一次好嗎？
Sasha 莎夏	I said let's get her to jump off that bridge. 我説讓她從橋上跳下去。
Joel 喬爾	No, it means nothing and it's also way over the top. 不，這一點意義都沒有，而且也太誇張了。
Sasha 莎夏	Frankly speaking, I think you are really judgmental and irresponsible! 坦白説，我覺得你很愛批評，又很不負責任！
Joel 喬爾	And you're very difficult! 妳才真的很龜毛！

60. saved by the bell　（在緊要關頭）得救

💬 **危機解除了：**

A: The teacher decided to give us a quiz, but then the bell rang.
老師本來準備給我們考試的，但是鐘聲響起來了。

B: You were saved by the bell!
所以你們在最後關頭得救了！

💬 **終於鬆一口氣：**

The meeting went on and on, and we were saved by the bell when the chairman was called away.
會議一直開一直開，我們在主席被叫走時得救了。

61. raise one's eyebrows　吃驚

💬 **無法置信：**

A: She raised her eyebrows when she heard that Tom got fired.
當她聽說湯姆被開除了，很驚訝！

B: I couldn't believe it myself, either.
我自己也不相信。

💬 **這是真的嗎：**

Mom raised her eyebrows when she heard that I had passed the exam.
媽媽聽說我通過了考試很驚訝！

* eye·brow	[ˋaɪˌbraʊ]	名	眉毛

62. keep one's head above water   使……免於負債

💬 **差強人意：**

A: How is your business?
你的公司經營得怎麼樣啊？

B: Just keeping my head above water.
剛剛好維持不負債而已。

💬 **量入為出的理財哲學：**

A: I have been trying to keep my head above water for the last year.
過去的一年裡我一直保持剛剛好不負債。

B: You are doing very well now.
你現在過得很好囉！

63. *bark* up the wrong tree
精力用在不該用的地方；錯怪人；目標錯誤

💬 **找錯目標：**

A: Can you lend me some money?
你可不可以借我一些錢？

B: Well, you are *barking* up the wrong tree.
你找錯人了。

💬 **想錯了：**

A: It seems that editing is easy.
當編輯似乎很容易。

B: If you are looking for an easy job, you are *baking* up the wrong tree.
你若是在找一個輕鬆的工作的話，你的目標就錯了。

* bark	[bɑrk]	動	（狗）吠叫

64. It's *sink* or swim.　無論成功或失敗（全靠自己）

💬 關鍵時刻：

A: It's *sink* or swim for Mary today.
今天是決定瑪莉存亡的日子了。

B: Is today her interview day?
今天是她的面試嗎？

💬 不成功便成仁：

A: You are on your own now. No one will help you.
你現在得靠你自己了。沒人會幫你喔。

B: I know, it's *sink* or swim.
我知道啊！我不是成功就是失敗囉。

* sink	[sɪŋk]	動	沉沒、沉

65. steal one's *thunder*　搶別人的功勞；竊取別人的方法

💬 不要搶我的風頭：

A: Hey, everyone! Do you know that Bill is getting married next month?
大家，你們知道下個月比爾要結婚了嗎？

B: Don't steal my *thunder*. I am going to tell people myself.
別搶了我的風采，我要自己告訴大家。

💬 功勞遭人竊取：

A: Why are you mad at Vivian?
你為什麼生薇薇安的氣！

B: Because she stole my *thunder*.
因為她搶了我的功勞。

* thun·der	[ˈθʌndə]	名	雷、打雷

66. Where there's *smoke*, there's fire.
無風不起浪；事出必有因。

💬 **案情並不單純：**

A: Do you believe the rumor that Terry and Mary are breaking up?
你相信泰瑞和瑪莉要分手的傳言嗎？

B: Where there is *smoke*, there is fire.
無風不起浪。

💬 **事情絕不會空穴來風：**

A: People are saying that our company has financial problemes.
大家都在說我們公司有財務上的困難。

B: Where there is *smoke*, there is is fire. We will probably find out very soon.
無風不起浪，我們應該很快就會知道了。

| * smoke | [smok] | 名 | 煙、煙塵 |

67. Knowledge is power. 知識就是力量。

💬 **學習是必需的：**

A: Why do we have to learn English?
我們為什麼要學英文啊？

B: Knowledge is power.
因為知識就是力量。

💬 **同樣的用法：**

A: Knowledge is power, which is why you should study more.
知識就是力量，所以你應該多讀一些書。

B: I know. I go to the library every week.
我知道，我每個禮拜都去圖書館。

Chapter 03 職場應對 *Business Conversation*

68. the bottom line is (that)...　基本底限；最終結果

💬 **最基本的要求：**

A: Do you know what our company's *operating* principles are?
你知道公司的營運方針是什麼嗎？

B: I'm not sure, but the bottom line is a good profit margin.
我不太清楚，但基本要求是有好的利潤。

💬 **結果顯而易見：**

A: We can earn money by selling these cups that we make.
我們可以賣我們做的這些杯子賺錢。

B: The bottom line is that we'd lose money selling them.
我們最後還是會賠錢的。

| * op·er·ate | [ˈɑpəˌret] | 動 | 運轉、操作 |

69. Time's up.　時間到了。

💬 **還沒準備好：**

A: Time's up.
時間到了。

B: But I'm not ready yet.
可是我還沒準備好。

💬 **請再多給一些時間：**

A: Time's up.
時間到了。

B: Can you wait awhile?
你可以等一下嗎？

💬 **考試時間結束了：**

Time's up. Please put your pens down.
時間到了，請停筆。

🐼 Chat 不斷流

Ariel 艾莉兒	Peter called in the middle of the night. 彼得半夜打給我。
Ren 仁恩	What was that about? 他説什麼？
Ariel 艾莉兒	I raised my eyebrows when he said he wanted to borrow ten thousand dollars. 他説要借一萬元時，我很吃驚！
Ren 仁恩	Yeah. That's a lot of money! 對啊，這不是小錢。
Ariel 艾莉兒	So, I told him that he is definitely barking up the wrong tree. 所以，我跟他説他找錯人了。
Ren 仁恩	How come? 為什麼？
Ariel 艾莉兒	I've been in debt before. And now I'm trying to keep my head above water. 我曾經負債，現在我試著讓自己不再欠錢。
Ren 仁恩	He might have brought this upon himself anyway. Where there's smoke, there's fire. 反正他很可能是咎由自取，事出必有因。
Ariel 艾莉兒	Exactly. The bottom line is that he needs to get himself together. 沒錯。底限就是他必須自己振作起來。
Ren 仁恩	Yeah. Maybe he should go back to school and finish his degree. 是啊，也許他該回學校完成學業。
Ariel 艾莉兒	That's right. Knowledge is power. 説得對，知識就是力量。

70. The sooner, the better.　越快越好。

🗨 早點回家比較好：

A: When should I come home?
我什麼時候該回到家？

B: The sooner, the better.
越快越好。

🗨 請盡速完成：

A: When do you want this mailed?
你什麼時候要寄這封信？

B: The sooner, the better.
越快越好。

🗨 能多快就多快：

I have to finish the project. The sooner, the better.
我必須要完成這個專案，越快越好。

71. If it sounds too good to be true, it probably is.
如果聽起來好的不像是真的，也許就不是真的。

🗨 好到讓人難以置信：

A: Are you kidding? They are *renting* their house for only $10000 a month?
你在開玩笑嗎？他們的房子一個月只租一萬元？

B: If it sounds too good to be true, it probably is.
如果聽起來好的不像是真的，也許就不是真的！

🗨 同樣的意思：

A: I am getting a raise. It sounds too good to be true.
我要加薪了，這聽起來太不可思議了！

B: If it sounds too good to be true, it probably is.
如果聽起來好的不像是真的，也許就不是真的！

* rent	[rɛnt]	動	租借

72. **It's not a big deal.** 沒什麼大不了的。

💬 再接再勵就好了：

A: I didn't pass my test.
我考試沒有通過。

B: It's not a big deal. Try harder next time.
沒什麼大不了的，下次努力點。

💬 小事一件：

A: I lost my hat.
我把我的帽子弄丟了。

B: It's not a big deal.
沒什麼大不了的。

💬 能解決就沒什麼好擔心的：

It's not a big deal. We can fix the problem soon.
沒什麼大不了的。我們可以盡快解決這個問題。

73. **Is it clear?** 清楚嗎？

💬 這眼鏡適合我嗎：

A: Let me try this pair of glasses.
讓我試試這副眼鏡。

B: Is it clear?
清楚嗎？

💬 搞清楚程序：

A: Please go to the counter for checking-in. Is it clear?
請到櫃檯辦理登機，清楚嗎？

B: Yes.
是的。

💬 明白了嗎：

The test will cover 3 chapters. Is it clear?
這次考試涵蓋了三個章節，清楚嗎？

74. point-blank　單刀直入地

💬 說話不拐彎抹角：

A: He told me point-blank to leave.
他很直接地叫我離開。

B: It's mind-boggling!
真是難以置信！

💬 直言不諱：

The boss told the employees point-blank that they are fired!
老闆單刀直入地跟員工說他們被開除了。

75. give someone a piece of one's mind　教訓某人一頓

💬 為人打抱不平：

A: Jimmy dumped me for another girl.
吉米為了另一個女人甩了我。

B: I am going to give him a piece of my mind. He is abominable.
我要去教訓他一頓！他實在太可惡了！

💬 教訓以示懲戒：

I am going to give Ryan a piece of my mind. How could he do such a thing?
我要教訓雷恩一頓，他怎麼可以做這種事！

76. bring home the bacon　維持生計；獲得成功

💬 男主外：

A: How could your mother have time for dancing?
你媽媽怎麼會有時間去跳舞？

B: My father is the one that brings home the bacon.
我爸爸是家裡維持生計的人。

💬 簽約成功就能加薪了：

If I bring home the bacon with this contract, I will get a raise.
如果這份計畫我簽成了，我就會被加薪。

77. **pull out all the stops**　用盡一切的實力

💬 卯足全力：

A: Will the project be finished on time?
　　這計畫會按時間做完嗎？

B: If we pull out all the stops.
　　如果我們發揮一切的實力。

💬 全力以赴：

A: Raymond pulled out all the stops while running the race.
　　雷蒙在跑步比賽中用盡一切實力。

B: No wonder he won.
　　難怪他贏得了比賽。

78. **shape up or ship out**　好自為之，不然就走路

💬 自己看著辦吧：

You are late again for practice. You better shape up or ship out.
你練習又遲到了！你最好好自為之，不然就走路！

💬 最後通碟：

You have been really sloppy these days: you better shape up or ship out.
你最近很懶散，你最好好自為之，不然就離開吧。

79. so quiet that you could hear a pin drop
安靜到連根針掉到地上都聽得見

💬 **全部的人都屏住呼吸：**

The conference room was so quiet that you could hear a pin drop.
會議室安靜地連一根針掉到地上都聽得見。

💬 **一點聲音都沒有：**

Everybody was so quiet that you could hear a pin drop when
Mrs. Brown screamed *silence*.
當布朗太太叫大家安靜時，大家安靜地連根針掉到地上都聽得見。

* si·lence	[ˋsaɪləns]	名	沉默

80. When the cat's away, the mice will play.
閻王不在，小鬼跳樑。

💬 **貓不在，老鼠就作怪：**

A: It seems that the employees in your company are not so
aggressive.
你們公司的員工似乎不是很有衝勁。

B: When the cat's away, the mice will play. Our director is on a
business trip this month.
閻王不在，小鬼跳樑，我們的主管這個月出差去了。

💬 **家裡沒大人：**

A: Mom and Dad are going to Europe next month.
爸爸媽媽下個月要去歐洲。

B: Wow! When the cat's away, the mice will play.
哇！閻王不在，小鬼跳樑。

* ag·gres·sive	[əˋgrɛsɪv]	形	有幹勁的、侵略的、攻擊的

📷 Chat 不斷流

Barbara 芭芭拉	When David comes, I'm going to give him a piece of my mind. 大衛一來，我就要好好教訓他。
Leo 里歐	Yeah. The sooner you let him know, the better. 沒錯，越早跟他說越好。
Barbara 芭芭拉	David, you've been coming in late recently. 大衛，你最近很常遲到。
David 大衛	It's not a big deal. 這又沒什麼大不了的。
Barbara 芭芭拉	Get it together if you still want to bring home the bacon! 如果你還想維持生計就好好表現。
David 大衛	For the record, this is only the third time I've been late this month. 正式地說，我這只是這個月第三次遲到。
Barbara 芭芭拉	Let me tell you point blank, David, shape up or ship out. Is it clear? 我直接跟你說，請你好自為之，不然就走路，清楚嗎？
David 大衛	Crystal clear. 極其明白。

Chapter 4

愛情滋味

All About Love

Chapter 04 音檔雲端連結

因各家手機系統不同，若無法直接掃描，
仍可以至以下電腦雲端連結下載收聽。
(https://tinyurl.com/y5mbbwmk)

🐾 Chat 聊不停

🎧 *Track 447*

01. have butterflies in one's stomach　緊張

💬 **見女友父母，心裡揣測不安：**

I am having butterflies in my stomach! I don't know whether my girlfriend's parents will like me or not.
我好緊張喔！我不知道我女朋友的爸媽會不會喜歡我！

💬 **緊要關頭壓力無法承受：**

A: I don't think I can make it to the finals. I am having butterflies in my stomach.
我想我沒辦法撐到決賽了，我好緊張喔！

B: Take it easy! I believe you can do it!
放輕鬆一點，我相信你可以做到的！

🎧 *Track 448*

02. Leave me alone.　別煩我。

💬 **愛情不來電：**

A: Hi! Want to go to the movies with me?
嗨！你要不要跟我一起去看電影？

B: Why don't you leave me alone?
你可不可以不要煩我？

💬 **實在提不起勁：**

A: Cheer up and go have some fun.
開心一點，去玩一下嘛！

B: Just leave me alone.
別煩我！

💬 **筋疲力盡，完全不想動：**

Leave me alone, please. I am so tired.
可不可以不要煩我，我覺得好累。

03. read between the lines　字裡行間的言外之意

💬 **愛意藏在字裡行間：**

A: What did he say in the letter?
他在信裡說了些什麼？

B: Nothing much, but I could read between the lines that he
misses me a lot.
沒什麼，但我由他的字裡行間看得出他真的很想我。

💬 **臆測他人的弦外之音：**

He was very careful with what he wrote. We had to read between
the lines to know what he meant.
他對他寫的東西很小心，我們必須揣摩他的話才知道他的意思。

04. head over heels　深陷；完全地

💬 **熱戀中：**

A: Amy seems to be in a good mood recently.
艾咪最近似乎心情很好。

B: It's because she's head over heels in love with Jimmy.
那是因為她與吉米在熱戀中。

💬 **無法脫困：**

Ted is troubled recently, for he is head over heels in *debt*.
泰德最近很煩惱，因為他深陷債務中。

* debt	[dɛt]	名	債、欠款

05. That's life. 這就是人生。

💬 **人生不如意十之八九：**

A: She got divorced and lost her job at the same time. I don't know what she is going to do.
她同時離婚又失業了，我真不知道她該怎麼辦？

B: I guess that's life. I hope she pulls herself together.
我想這就是人生！我希望她重新振作起來。

💬 **過河拆橋：**

A: I helped her through all her difficulties and now she turns her back on me.
我幫助她度過許多難關，現在她卻不理我！

B: That's life!
這就是人生！

06. Money talks. 金錢萬能。

💬 **愛情輸給了現實：**

A: She married the old man for his *fortune*.
她因為那老人的財產而嫁給他。

B: Money talks.
金錢是萬能的。

💬 **有錢能使鬼推磨：**

A: How did you persuade him to help you?
你怎麼說服他幫你的？

B: Money talks.
金錢是萬能的。

* for·tune	[ˈfɔrtʃən]	名	運氣、財富

07. not one's cup of tea 　不合興趣；不合胃口

💬 抱歉！那不是我的菜：

A: How about going to the rock concert with me?
你要不要跟我一起去搖滾音樂會？

B: No, thanks. Rock concert is not my cup of tea.
不了，謝謝！搖滾樂不合我的胃口。

💬 環境造就個性：

A: Living in the country is not Jenny's cup of tea.
鄉下的生活不適合珍妮。

B: She is more of a city girl.
她是一個城市女孩。

08. in short 　總而言之

💬 總之情已逝：

A: In short, Sally doesn't love Ted anymore.
總而言之，莎麗已經不愛泰德了。

B: No wonder she is filing for a *divorce*.
難怪她在申請離婚。

💬 無論如何，旅行是很棒的：

A: So how was your trip to London?
你的倫敦之旅如何啊？

B: It was great in short.
總而言之，很棒就是了。

💬 不想多說：

It was good in short.
總而言之就是很好。

* di·vorce	[də`vors]	名	離婚、解除婚約

09. Do it.　動手去做；去做吧！

愛要即時：

A: I'm fond of Mia. I'd love to have a movie date with her.
我很喜歡蜜亞，想約她看電影。

B: Just do it!
那就去呀！

沒什麼好猶豫的：

A: I want to move out of my house.
我想要搬出家裡。

B: Do it.
去做吧！

一定要做就對了：

Either you or I do it.
不是你做就是我做。

10. Shut up.　別吵了。

鬧脾氣，不講道理：

A: Shut up. Stop making trouble out of nothing!
別吵了，不要再無理取鬧了！

B: You don't love me anymore.
你不愛我了。

噓！保持安靜：

A: Shut up. This is a library.
別吵了，這裡是圖書館。

B: Sorry about that.
抱歉。

專心聽話：

Shut up and listen here.
閉嘴，聽這邊。

Chapter 04 愛情滋味 All About Love

🐼 Chat 不 斷 流

Mason 麥森	Man, let's go get a drink tonight. 兄弟，晚上我們去喝一杯吧！
Lucas 盧卡斯	Leave me alone. I'm really depressed right now. 別煩我，我現在很沮喪！
Mason 麥森	What happened? 發生什麼事了？
Lucas 盧卡斯	Lucy just sent me a text. I read between the lines and realized that she wants to date another rich dude. 露西剛發了一封訊息給我，從她的字裡行間我感覺出她想和另一個有錢人交往。
Mason 麥森	Money talks! 果然金錢萬能呀！
Lucas 盧卡斯	Yeah... I guess that's life. 唉，也許這就是人生！
Mason 麥森	Don't be sad. Maybe you're just not Lucy's cup of tea. 別難過！也許露西不適合你。
Lucas 盧卡斯	But I'm head over heels for her. I'm having butterflies in my stomach. I'm scared that Lucy is going to dump me. 但我已經深陷其中了。所以，我很緊張，很怕露西要分手。
Mason 麥森	Don't worry. Just wait and see! 先別擔心，靜觀其變吧！
Lucas 盧卡斯	That's easy for you to say. 説得比較容易。

11. **Don't bother me.**　別打擾我（當自己很忙時）。

💬 **好心沒好報：**

A: Babe, what's up?
　　親愛的，怎麼了？

B: Don't bother me.
　　別打擾我。

💬 **不要吵我：**

A: You look very busy.
　　你看起來很忙。

B: Yes, don't bother me.
　　對啊！別打擾我。

💬 **也可以這樣說：**

Don't bother me at the moment, please.
現在請不要打擾我。

12. **What have you been up to lately?**　最近忙些什麼？

💬 **忙到昏天暗地：**

A: Babe, I'm sorry. I have been very busy lately.
　　寶貝，對不起，我最近很忙。

B: What have you been up to lately?
　　最近忙些什麼？

💬 **事出必有因：**

A: I have not been to school for a long time.
　　我很久沒去學校了。

B: What have you been up to lately?
　　最近忙些什麼？

Chapter **04** 愛情滋味 *All About Love*

13. have second thoughts　考慮一下；猶豫

💬 **終身大事要慎重其事：**

A: Congratulations! You are getting married this summer.
恭喜！你今年夏天就要結婚了！

B: Well, I am having second thoughts. I don't know if I am ready yet.
我在猶豫了，我不知道我準備好了沒。

💬 **買車不是小事：**

I am having second thoughts about buying that car.
我還得再考慮一下要不要買那部車。

14. Is there anything wrong?　有問題嗎？

💬 **發生什麼事：**

A: I'm not getting married with Eric.
我不會和艾瑞克結婚了。

B: Why? Is there anything wrong?
怎麼了？有什麼問題嗎？

💬 **不滿意要退貨：**

A: I want my money back!
我要退錢。

B: Why? Is there anything wrong?
為什麼？有什麼問題嗎？

💬 **到底怎麼了：**

Is there anything wrong? Please tell me.
有什麼問題嗎？請告訴我。

15. Calm down.　冷靜一點。

💬 **沒什麼大不了的：**

A: Calm down. You'll meet a better man.
冷靜一點，下一個男人會更好。

B: But he's the only one I love.
但我只愛他。

💬 **太衝動，後果自負：**

A: You had better calm down, or you will get into trouble.
你最好冷靜一點，不然你就有麻煩了。

B: Are you *threatening* me?
你在恐嚇我嗎？

💬 **試圖讓自己冷靜以對：**

I tried to calm down when I heard the bad news.
聽到這個壞消息時我嘗試著冷靜。

* threat·en	[ˈθrɛtn̩]	動	威脅

🎧 *Track 463*

16. **behind someone's back**　在某人背後；背著某人……

💬 **對感情不忠實：**

He went out with Rebecca behind his girlfriend's back.
他背著他女朋友和麗貝嘉出去約會。

💬 **別在背後說人閒話了：**

It isn't fair to talk behind Lisa's back.
在麗莎的背後說她是不公平的。

🎧 *Track 464*

17. **let someone off the hook**　讓某人擺脫麻煩、解脫困境

💬 **不要再有下一次了：**

A: Did you yell at John for his being late?
約翰遲到了，妳有沒有生氣？

B: No, I let him off the hook this time, and made him promise never to be late again.
我這次饒了他，並要他答應下一次不可以再遲到了！

💬 **離我遠一點：**

Would you stop asking questions and let me off the hook?
你可不可以不要再問我問題了，別再煩我了。

Track 465

18. Out of sight, out of mind.　眼不見為淨；離久情疏。

相看兩相厭：

A: Why are you throwing away John's letter?
你為什麼把約翰給你的信都丟了？

B: Out of sight, out of mind. We broke up yesterday.
眼不見為淨，我們昨天分手了。

人是善忘的：

A: I don't want to go on a tour to promote my new book!
我不想巡迴去介紹我的新書。

B: Out of sight, out of mind.
他們沒看到你就會忘了你的！

Track 466

19. be fed up with...　對……感到厭煩

再也受不了了：

A: Why did Mary leave Jack?
瑪麗為什麼離開傑克？

B: Mary is fed up with his lies.
她已經受夠了他的謊話了。

可以換個新環境了：

I am so fed up with my job. I want to change jobs.
我對我的工作感到厭煩，我想換工作了。

Track 467

20. accidentally/on purpose　不小心／故意

無心之下發現的事：

I accidentally saw her letter to John, and found out they are going to get married soon.
我不小心看到她寫給約翰的信，發現他們快要結婚了。

要引人注意：

He slipped and fell over on purpose in front of her to get her *attention*.
他故意在她面前跌倒，以引起她的注意。

252

| * at·ten·tion | [ə`tenʃən] | 名 | 注意、專心 |

Ava 愛娃	Hey Emma. What have you been up to lately? 艾瑪，最近在忙些什麼？
Emma 艾瑪	As usual. Nothing special. 就跟往常一樣，沒什麼特別。
Ava 愛娃	I heard you're getting married soon. Congratulations! 聽說妳快要結婚了，恭喜呀！
Emma 艾瑪	I'm having second thoughts. 我還要再考慮一下。
Ava 愛娃	Is there anything wrong? 有什麼問題嗎？
Emma 艾瑪	A while ago, I accidentally found out that my fiancé is contacting his ex-girlfriend behind my back. I'm so mad! 前一陣子，我不小心發現我未婚夫竟背著我跟前女友聯絡，我很生氣！
Ava 愛娃	Calm down. Maybe it's nothing. 冷靜一點！也許根本沒什麼。
Emma 艾瑪	That's what he said. I let him off the hook this time, but I am so fed up with this kind of thing. 他也這麼說，所以，這次饒了他。但，我對這種事感到厭煩。
Ava 愛娃	Most women hate it. 大部份的女生都不喜歡的。

Chapter **04** 愛情滋味 *All About Love*

21. It's the thought that counts. 心意最重要。

💬 **禮輕情意重：**

A: I was thinking about buying you a gold ring, but I didn't have enough money. So, I bought you a bouquet of flowers instead.
我本來想為你買一個金戒指，但是我沒有足夠的錢，所以我只買了一束花。

B: That's OK. It's the thought that counts.
沒關係，心意最重要。

💬 **心意到就好：**

A: I bought you some bread, but I forgot it on the bus.
我幫你買了一些麵包，但是我把它忘在公車上了。

B: It's the thought that counts. I am not hungry anyway.
心意最重要，反正我也不餓。

22. through thick and thin 同甘共苦

💬 **愛讓他們不離不棄：**

They have stick with each other through thick and thin. I think they will never leave each other.
他們在一起經歷了很多事，我想他們是不會分開了吧。

💬 **相知相守：**

I know him very well because we have been through thick and thin together.
我很了解他，因為我們在一起經歷了很多事。

23. **It takes two to tango.** 一個巴掌拍不響。

💬 兩個人都有問題：

A: My boyfriend is always *nagging* me.
　　我的男朋友一天到晚都在唸我！

B: Well, it takes two to tango.
　　一個巴掌拍不響。

💬 太無禮了：

A: You shouldn't have said that to make mom angry.
　　你剛剛不應該那樣說話惹媽媽生氣！

B: It takes two to tango, you know.
　　你知道那不只是我一個人的錯。

* nag	[næg]	動	使煩惱、嘮叨

24. **Talk is *cheap*.** 光說沒有用。

💬 真愛要付諸行動：

A: I really love you. I could give you anything.
　　我真很愛你，我可以給你任何東西。

B: Talk is *cheap*. Actions speak for themselves.
　　光沒說有用，行動可以證明一切。

💬 坐而言不如起而行：

A: I am going to make a lot of money!
　　我要賺很多錢。

B: Talk is *cheap*. Show me!
　　光說沒有用，證明給我看啊！

* cheap	[tʃip]	形	低價的、易取得的

Chapter 04 愛情滋味 *All About Love*

25. Opposites *attract*.　異性相吸。

💬 愛情沒有什麼道理：

A: How could a city girl like you love a country boy like him?
一個像妳一樣的都市女孩怎會喜歡一個鄉村男孩？

B: Opposites *attract*.
異性相吸囉！

💬 跌破眾人眼鏡：

A: I didn't think that people as different as Joe and Mary could be so happily married.
我以前不認為像喬和瑪莉那麼不同的兩個人可以有這麼幸福的婚姻。

B: I think so. But they say, opposites *attract*.
我也這麼認為，不過他們說異性相吸。

* at·tract	[əˈtrækt]	動	吸引

26. a wolf in sheep's clothing　披著羊皮的狼

💬 真心換絕情：

A: My girlfriend ran away with my best friend.
我的女朋友和我最要好的朋友跑了。

B: Well, I guess he is a wolf in sheep's clothing.
嗯，我想他是一個披著羊皮的狼。

💬 貌若天仙，心如蛇蠍：

A: I thought she was a nice girl, but now I know I was wrong.
我以為她是一個好女孩，可是現在我知道我錯了。

B: She is a wolf in sheep's clothing.
她是披著羊皮的狼。

27. The best things in life are free.
生命中最好的東西是金錢買不到的。

💬 愛情價更高：

A: I love him even though he has no money.
縱使他沒有錢，我還是愛他。

B: The best things in life are free.
生命中最好的東西是金錢買不到的。

💬 再多錢也買不到：

A: Isn't that view *gorgeous*?
這個景色是不是很迷人？

B: Yup. The best things in life are free.
是啊！生命中最好的東西是金錢買不到的。

| * gor·geous | [ˈgɔrdʒəs] | 形 | 炫麗的、極好的 |

28. What's even worse... 更慘的是⋯⋯

💬 壞事接二連三：

A: Tony failed the exam.
湯尼沒通過考試。

B: What's even worse is that his girlfriend wants to break up with him.
更慘的是，他的女朋友想跟他分手。

💬 禍不單行：

A: A dog bit Joe yesterday.
昨天有一隻狗咬了喬。

B: Yeah. What's even worse is that a car hit him on his way to the hospital.
對啊！更慘的是，在他去醫院的途中他又被車撞到。

💬 還有更糟糕的：

What's even worse is that he doesn't know why he is wrong.
更慘的是，他不知道他錯在哪。

Chapter *04* 愛情滋味 *All About Love*

29. I still have things to do.　我還有事要做。

💬 **還不能休息呀：**

A: Honey, let's go out for a walk.
親愛的，我們一起出去走走吧。

B: Sorry, I still have things to do.
對不起，我還有事要做。

💬 **時間緊迫：**

A: Why are you in a rush?
你為什麼那麼急？

B: I still have things to do.
我還有事要做。

💬 **要走了，不能再擔誤了：**

I need to leave now. I still have things to do.
我現在要離開了，我還有事情要做。

30. Only time will tell.　只有時間能證明一切。

💬 **讓我們拭目以待吧：**

A: Do you think they will be happy getting married so early?
你覺得他們那麼早結婚會開心嗎？

B: Who knows? Only time will tell.
誰知道？只有時間能證明一切。

💬 **未來很難說：**

A: Did we make the right decision on sending our son abroad?
我們把兒子送到國外去是做對了決定嗎？

B: I hope so, but only time will tell.
我希望囉！但是只有時間能證明一切。

🐱 Chat 不 斷 流

Ethan 伊森	Mia, why did you accept my proposal? 蜜亞，妳為什麼會答應嫁給我？
Mia 蜜亞	Because opposites attract! 因為異性相吸呀！
Ethan 伊森	Don't joke. Be serious. 不要開玩笑！說認真的。
Mia 蜜亞	I was once told that you are a wolf in sheep's clothing. People told me to be careful, but I realized that you are not like that. 曾經有人說，你是披著羊皮的狼，叫我要小心！但是，我發現其實你不是這樣的。
Ethan 伊森	I see. 我知道了。
Mia 蜜亞	What's even worse is that my parents also disagreed at the time. 更慘的是，當時我父母也反對。
Ethan 伊森	Only time will tell. You've got to believe me. 時間自會證明一切，妳要相信我。
Mia 蜜亞	Talk is cheap. You better work hard so we can have a good life. 光說沒有用，你可要努力，讓我們過幸福的生活。
Ethan 伊森	Trust me. You won't regret marrying me. 相信我，妳不會後悔嫁給我的。
Mia 蜜亞	We will work through thick and thin together. 我們會一起同甘共苦。

Chapter 04 愛情滋味 *All About Love*

259

31. I have had enough!　我真是受夠了！

💬 分道揚鑣，不再委曲求全：

A: Why are you breaking up with him?
你為什麼要和他分手？

B: I have had enough of his bad temper.
我真是受夠了他的壞脾氣。

💬 爆炸了，不想忍了：

A: I have had enough!
我真是受夠了！

B: Why? What did he do?
為什麼？他做了什麼？

💬 忍無可忍：

I have had enough of the *noise*.
我受夠了噪音。

| * noise | [nɔɪz] | 名 | 喧鬧聲、噪音 |

32. That's the last *straw*.　再也無法忍受。

💬 最後一根稻草：

A: Karen decided to leave Kurt last night.
凱倫昨晚決定離開柯特。

B: They have been having problems, but Kurt having an affair with his secretary was the last *straw*.
他們之間一直都有問題，但是柯特和他祕書的婚外情終於使凱倫再也無法忍受。

💬 致命的一擊：

He was very upset about being fired, and his wife leaving him was the last *straw*.
他被開除已經很難過了，而他太太離開他，終於使他再也無法忍受。

| * straw | [strɔ] | 名 | 稻草 |

33. On the *contrary*,...　相反地，……

💬 意外的結果：

A: So did they get married ？
你們結婚了嗎？

B: On the *contrary*, they broke up.
相反地，他們分手了。

💬 一點都不好玩：

A: Did you have a good time at the party?
你們在派對上好玩嗎？

B: No, on the *contrary*, it was boring.
相反地，好無聊。

💬 竟然如此：

I didn't go to Japan last month. On the *contrary*, I stayed at home.
上個月我沒有去日本。相反地，我待在家裡。

| * con·trar·y | [ˈkɑntrɛrɪ] | 名 | 矛盾 |

34. There are other fish in the sea.　還有別的機會。

💬 失去了一棵樹還有一座林：

A: What am I going to do without Sara?
我失去了莎拉怎麼辦？

B: There are other fish in the sea. You will find the love of your life someday.
天涯何處無芳草，何必單戀一枝花？你總有一天會找到你的摯愛的。

💬 會有更好的選擇：

A: I didn't get the job.
我沒被錄取。

B: There are other fish in the sea. Don't worry!
還有別的機會，別擔心！

Chapter 04 愛情滋味 All About Love

261

35. **Now you know!**　你現在才知道！

💬 **原來是這樣的啊：**

A: That's why you don't like him.
所以妳會不喜歡他。

B: Now you know!
你現在才知道！

💭 **沒知識也要有常識：**

A: So the earth is round?
所以地球是圓的？

B: Now you know.
你現在才知道？

💬 **講清楚，說明白：**

Now you know! She is not a good person.
現在你知道了，她不是好人。

36. **like a dream come true**　如夢成真

💬 **終於如願以償：**

A: I heard that Mike has finally proposed to you.
我聽說麥克終於跟你求婚了！

B: Yes, it's like a dream come true.
是的，這真是美夢成真！

💭 **不再是痴心妄想了：**

I have finally defeated our *opponents*. It's like a dream come true.
我終於打敗我們的對手了！這真是美夢成真！

* op·po·nent	[ə`ponənt]	名	對手、反對者

37. from the bottom of one's heart　由衷地；真心地

💬 **掏心掏肺的真愛：**

A: I love my boyfriend from the bottom of my heart.
我是真心的愛我的男朋友。

B: You guys seem to be the happiest couple in the world.
你們似乎是世界上最開心的一對。

💬 **肺腑之言：**

A: You must be really *grateful* that they found your cat!
你一定很感激他們幫你找回貓咪！

B: I am *grateful* from the bottom of my heart.
我是由衷地感謝。

＊ grate·ful	[ˈgretfəl]	形	感激的、感謝的

38. Love is blind.　愛情是盲目的。

💬 **情人眼裡出西施：**

A: Peter is not very handsome, but Sarah thinks he is the most gorgeous guy in the world.
彼得並不很帥，但莎拉卻覺得他是世界上最帥的人了。

B: Love is blind.
愛情是盲目的。

💬 **愛到卡慘死：**

A: Although he is very mean to her, she married him anyway.
縱使他對她非常不好，她還是跟他結婚了。

B: Love is blind.
愛情是盲目的。

Chapter 04 愛情滋味 All About Love

39. How could you think that?　你怎麼可以這麼想？

💬 **疑心易生暗鬼：**

A: You don't love me anymore.
你不再愛我了。

B: How could you think that?
妳怎麼可以這麼想。

💬 **猜忌是愛情的毒藥：**

A: Are you in love with another man?
妳是不是愛上別的男人了？

B: How could you think that?
你怎麼可以這麼想？

40. Bad news travels fast.　壞事傳千里。

💬 **事情很容易就傳開了：**

A: Do you know Mary has divorced her busband?
你知道瑪莉和她先生離婚了嗎？

B: Yes, bad news travels fast.
我聽說了，壞事總是傳千里。

💬 **原來大家都知道：**

A: How did you know that Bob got fired?
你怎麼知道巴布被開除了？

B: Bad news travels fast.
壞事傳千里。

🐱 Chat 不斷流

Sophia 蘇菲亞	Oh, Ada, my friend. Are you alright? 哦，愛達，我的朋友，妳還好嗎？
Ada 愛達	You also heard that I got a divorce? Bad news surely travels fast. I'm just such a failure, right? 妳也聽到我離婚的消息了？真是壞事傳千里！我很失敗，對吧？
Sophia 蘇菲亞	How could you think that? On the contrary, I think you're very brave. 妳怎麼可以這麼想！相反地，我覺得妳很勇敢。
Ada 愛達	What was wrong with me? I thought getting married with him would be like a dream come true! 當初我是怎麼了？以為嫁給他是美夢成真了。
Sophia 蘇菲亞	Love is blind. It happens to everyone. 愛情是盲目的，在誰身上都會發生。
Ada 愛達	I've had enough of his bad temper. I was very unhappy after getting married. 他的壞脾氣，我真是受夠了！結婚後，我過得很不開心。
Sophia 蘇菲亞	Don't be sad. It's all over now. You can start over. There are other fish in the sea. 別難過，都結束了，妳還可以重新開始，還有別的機會的。
Ada 愛達	No, I want to stay single for now. 不！我想暫時一個人。
Sophia 蘇菲亞	Nevertheless, from the bottom of my heart, I wish you find happiness. 無論如何，我由衷地希望妳找到幸福。
Ada 愛達	Thank you, Sophia. I'm so lucky to have you as my friend. 謝謝妳，蘇菲亞，有妳這朋友真好！

Chapter 04 愛情滋味 *All About Love*

41. **Beauty is in the eye of the beholder.**　情人眼裡出西施。

💬 **愛情是盲目的：**

A: Sara is so beautiful!
莎拉真是美麗！

B: Beauty is in the eye of the beholder.
情人眼裡出西施。

💬 **愛情不能比較：**

A: I think Missy's boyfriend is not good enough for her.
我覺得米西的男朋友配不上她。

B: Beauty is in the eye of the beholder.
情人眼裡出西施。

42. *Absence* **makes the heart grow fonder.**
距離反而拉近彼此的感情；小別勝新婚。

💬 **偶爾分開更有吸引力：**

Absence makes the heart grow fonder. We have been closer than before since Sam returned from his business trip.
小別勝新婚！自從山姆出差回來後，我們比以前更親近了呢！

💬 **距離有時是一種美感：**

A: I really miss my brother. He is studying in Canada.
我真的很想念我弟弟，他在加拿大讀書。

B: *Absence* makes the heart grow fonder. You guys used to fight a lot.
距離反而拉近彼此的感情，你們以前還常常吵架呢！

* ab·sence	[ˈæbsn̩s]	名	缺席、缺乏

43. like two peas in a pod   膩在一起

💬 **每天都是熱戀期：**

A: Sharon and Samuel are like two peas in a pod.
莎朗和山姆爾常常膩在一起。

B: They love each other very much.
他們彼此很相愛。

💬 **就愛黏著你：**

A: You have been spending a lot of time with Jimmy.
妳最近和吉姆常常在一起。

B: Yes, we are like two peas in a pod lately.
是的，我們最近常常膩在一起。

44. Two's company, three is a *crowd*.   兩人成伴，三人不歡。

💬 **才不要當電燈泡呢：**

A: Do you want to go with us to the movies?
你要不要跟我們一起去看電影？

B: No, two's company, three is a *crowd*.
不了，兩人成伴，三人不歡。

💬 **換個說法：**

A: So did you go to the party with Mary and Joe?
你有沒有跟瑪莉和喬去參加派對？

B: No, I didn't. Two's company, three is a *crowd*.
我沒有，因為兩人成伴，三人不歡。

| * crowd | [kraʊd] | 名 | 人群、群眾 |

Chapter 04 愛情滋味 All About Love

45. They lived happily ever after.
他們從此過著幸福快樂的日子。

💬 **如童話故事一般：**

A: They got married and...
他們結婚了，而且……

B: I know! And they lived happily ever after.
我知道，他們從此過著幸福快樂的日子。

💬 **美好的結局：**

A: So what happened to the characters in the movie?
電影裡面的人物最後怎麼了？

B: They lived happily ever after.
他們從此過著幸福快樂的日子了。

46. The third time's the *charm*. 第三次總是幸運的。

💬 **一定能成功：**

A: So, is this your third girlfriend? The third time's the *charm*.
這是你第三個女朋友啊？第三次總是幸運的！

B: Yeah, I hope to marry her someday. I really love her.
是的，我希望有一天可以跟她結婚，我真的很愛她。

💬 **要有信心，再試一次：**

A: I have tried to call him twice and I still can't reach him.
我已經試著打兩次電話給他了，但我還是找不到他。

B: Try it one more time. The third time's the *charm*.
再試一次看看，第三次總是幸運的。

| * charm | [tʃɑrm] | 名 | 魅力 |

47. **turn back the clock** 時間倒轉

💬 **浪子回頭，為時不晚：**

A: I wish I could turn back the clock and ask Kerry back.
我真希望可以倒轉時間，讓凱莉回到我身邊。

B: It is not too late now.
現在不算太晚啊！

💬 **感嘆時不我予：**

A: I wish I had saved more money.
我希望我過去有存一些錢。

B: There is no turning back the clock.
時間沒辦法倒轉囉！

🐾 Chat 不斷流

Jack 傑克	Abel, I'm having dinner with my girlfriend tonight. Wanna come? 阿貝，晚上我跟女朋友吃飯，你想來嗎？
Abel 阿貝	Nah, two's company, three is a crowd. 不了，兩人成伴、三人不歡。
Jack 傑克	Don't be dramatic! 別這麼誇張！
Abel 阿貝	I'm not interested in being the third wheel. 我不想當電燈泡。
Jack 傑克	She and I are always like two peas in a pod. We'll be fine. 我和她常常膩在一起，沒關係的。
Abel 阿貝	I'm so jealous. If I had your good looks, I won't keep failing my relationships! 好羨慕你呀！我如果像你一樣有型，戀愛就不會總是失敗了。
Jack 傑克	Beauty is in the eye of the beholder. Don't give up. The third time's the charm. 情人眼裡出西施，不要放棄，第三次總是幸運的！
Abel 阿貝	I also want a fairy tale relationship. She and I would be like a prince and a princess... 我也好想像故事裡的王子和公主一樣……
Jack 傑克	And they lived happily ever after. 他們從此過著幸福快樂的日子。
Abel 阿貝	That's what I'm talking about, brother! 就是這樣！兄弟。

語研力 **E093**

生活英語：
chit-chat 聊不停，聽力會話好流利

作　　　者	王洛媛	
顧　　　問	曾文旭	
出版總監	陳逸祺、耿文國	
主　　　編	陳薫芳	
執行編輯	翁芯琍	
美術編輯	李依靜	
法律顧問	北辰著作權事務所	

印　　　製	世和印製企業有限公司
初　　　版	2024 年 01 月
出　　　版	凱信企業集團 - 凱信企業管理顧問有限公司
電　　　話	（02）2773-6566
傳　　　真	（02）2778-1033
地　　　址	106 台北市大安區忠孝東路四段 218 之 4 號 12 樓
信　　　箱	kaihsinbooks@gmail.com

定　　　價	新台幣 349 元 / 港幣 116 元
產品內容	1 書

總 經 銷	采舍國際有限公司
地　　　址	235 新北市中和區中山路二段 366 巷 10 號 3 樓
電　　　話	（02）8245-8786
傳　　　真	（02）8245-8718

國家圖書館出版品預行編目資料

生活英語：chic-chat聊不停，聽力會話好流利／王
洛媛著. – 初版. – 臺北市：凱信企業集團凱信企業
管理顧問有限公司, 2024.01
　　面；　公分
ISBN 978-626-7354-25-4(平裝)

1.CST: 英語 2.CST: 會話